LEKKING BRE

In the NCO's mess Corporal Gunnersbury was preparing a punch which, he was confident, would set the seal of social success on the highland dancing. He worked happily emptying almost the entire reserve liquor stocks of the mess into a cookhouse dixie.

The punch had acquired a terrible pink potency. It bubbled like the surface of a soda lake. To top it all off, Corporal Gunnersbury heaved in some sliced lemons and a clove of garlic for luck, praying that these wouldn't dissolve, like portions of a corpse in an acid bath, before he could serve the mixture to the delighted dancers . . .

In the Rut

COLIN WILLOCK

SPHERE BOOKS LIMITED
30-32 Gray's Inn Road, London WC1X 8JL

First published in Great Britain by Sphere Books Ltd 1982

TRADE
MARK

Set in Lasercomp Times

Printed and bound in Great Britain by
©ollins, Glasgow

For my first grandchild, Mark,
living proof that the old system still works best.

August

'This afternoon,' said Captain Bertram Pomona, Officer Commanding Radar Tracking Unit, Island of Horn, North-West Scotland, 'I intend to carry out an unofficial inspection of operational equipment.'

'Great!' said his second-in-command, crossing and uncrossing a pair of legs that were rumoured to start immediately beneath her lieutenant's pips. Lieutenant Myfanwy Preece and Captain Pomona were alone in the orderly room.

'When, or rather where, or do I mean both, do you wish to start?'

Captain Pomona experienced a feeling of faintness centred on the nape of his neck. He got it whenever he was forced to look at, or even away from, the flashing-eyed Myfanwy's even more flashing legs.

'Lieutenant Preece,' he said firmly. 'I am concerned with this unit's key role in the early warning system of the NATO powers rather than with any personal alliance that may, or may not, exist between us in off-duty hours . . .'

'Pompous bastard,' he added reproachfully to himself.

Lieutenant Preece leapt to her feet and saluted.

'Oh God,' thought Pomona, noticing the way this standard, if exaggerated, military courtesy elevated the tip-tilt of her missile-like right breast five degrees above the angle of its twin. 'Oh God,' he thought, 'she bloody well did that on purpose.'

'Anything particular you wish to inspect, sir?'

'Oh do shut up, Myfanwy.'

Myfanwy Preece cut her right hand away sharply, knowing that her frontal aspect would return to the at-ease position with commendable military precision after an interesting moment or two of directional indecision.

Captain Pomona averted his eyes. He was a diligent

officer and skilled technician who loved his work. Lately he had been increasingly feeling that the over-charged atmosphere of his isolated half-male, half-female command had been getting too much for him.

'I'll start at the cookhouse,' he announced. As far as he could recall there was no operational radar equipment in the cookhouse. Nevertheless, sexwise, it seemed a good neutral place to begin.

Lunch had been over an hour. Tea was still two hours away. There was no reason why anything should have been going on in the cookhouse. Indeed, there was every reason why it shouldn't.

Captain Pomona noted with pleasure that the cooks' health certificates were prominently displayed inside the door. Privates Mary Cassidy, and Doris Bond were, he read, warranted free from contagious diseases. The cookhouse was one area of his command where he had every right to expect passion not to reign. For one thing, Private Cassidy was not everyone's cup of tea. She wasn't called 'Butch' merely in honour of the well-known outlaw. She was built like a front-row forward. Her assistant, Private 'Hideous 007' Bond was so dramatically ugly that she ought to have been safe from sexual assault, even on Horn. The 'Hideous' part of her nickname needed no explanation. Had she been born in medieval Paris, she could have stood in for a gargoyle on Notre Dame and might even have given Quasimodo a bad turn. The prefix 007 referred to the fact that her suet roll was said to be licensed to kill.

Pomona paused apprehensively. Laughter, dark as brown Windsor soup blended with a giggle as shrill as the grating of a knife (cook's) on the base of a kettle (camp, oval) echoed from behind the pantry door.

Pomona pushed the door open nervously, and with good reason.

Fingers lovingly entwined around the handle of a wooden spoon, the two cooks were rapturously stirring a bowl of spotted dick. The glances which each bestowed on the other were warm enough to scald the cauldron of porridge which stood nearby, like ready-mixed concrete, prepared for tomorrow's breakfast.

Neither cook appeared to notice him. Pomona slammed the door and fled. Was it his imagination or had the rot penetrated to the remotest recesses of his command?

It *must* be his imagination. Islands, it was well-known, did strange things to people. Look at Lesbos and poor old Sapho! He shuddered, remembering the cooks. Captain Pomona strode decisively on towards the next stop on his tour of inspection.

The radar tracking aerials stood on top of a small grassy mound, around whose base grew a thick screen of gorse bushes.

It was not the sort of bower he himself would have chosen as a trysting place. It is possible that orderly room clerk Mavis Prendergast and Lance-Corporal Mason saw some defensive value in it. It was obvious that they hadn't expected to be disturbed in the space they had cleared among the gorsey spines and spikes. It was equally obvious that the foot Captain Pomona so nearly deposited in the small of the Lance-Corporal's naked, sunburnt back hadn't distracted either of them from the business in hand.

'*Oops!* Sorry,' said Pomona and withdrew hastily. He couldn't think of anything else to say in the circumstances. They were both off duty. All the same they might have selected somewhere, well, less operational.

For a moment Captain Pomona considered paying a surprise visit to the duty radar watch. But what if they, too, were concentrating on things other than the possibility that the Russkis might choose this precise moment to launch a crafty intercontinental ballistic missile? Supposing his detachment was the one that caused the West to be caught, figuratively speaking, with its pants down? What if his radar watch had *their* pants down? Naturally, it was unthinkable that such a thing could happen. But, in his present highly overwrought state of mind, he found it increasingly hard to *un*think it. He decided not to chance things. He would give the duty watch a miss and drop in on the equipment store instead.

It was dark in the equipment store. Pomona found the

switch, but a strange and ominous sound stopped him abruptly from turning on the lights. One of the spare parabolic aerials was moving under its own power, producing a rhythmic metallic creaking as if tracking a heavenly body. The only question in Pomona's mind was: whose?

Captain Pomona would have liked to have put it all down to mice. In his heart he knew that not even Horn mice, however enthusiastic, made that kind of noise. Pomona took a deep breath and put the lights on.

His impressions in the few seconds before he turned them off again were confused. Later, he seemed to recall the parabolic aerial swinging violently upwards through ninety degrees and hurling a half naked female form on to a pile of camouflage netting.

Captain Pomona did not wait for further evidence of his command's total moral collapse. For the third time that afternoon, he made a strategic withdrawal.

He was only just in time. The crash from the equipment store had alerted CSM Markham who came running from his quarters to see what, or possibly who, was up.

Captain Pomona increasingly felt that matters were reaching a point at which he might no longer be able to overlook them. Next morning, in the orderly room, his worst fears were realised.

'What do you propose to charge them with, Sergeant-Major?' Captain Pomona sounded desperate.

'Improper use of, and causing damage to, War Department property by Corporal Gunnersbury and Private Stopham. In the equipment store, sir. On an Aerial Parabolic, Mark Two.'

'Apt,' agreed Pomona thoughtfully, 'but I doubt if they did much damage. Those parabolic aerials are awfully strong.'

'So is Corporal Gunnersbury, sir. Dirty great brute.'

Captain Pomona strongly suspected that CSM Markham had recently been rebuffed by Private Gwladys Stopham.

He made a determined attempt to head his Sergeant-Major off.

'Speaking man to man, CSM, the Ministry of Defence must have had something of this sort in mind when they took the inspired course of insisting that the Radar Tracking Unit should be composed half and half of men and women . . . Sort of Noah's Ark, if you get me.'

'A bit too much like it, I'm afraid, sir. They're overdoing the two-by-two bit.'

'Quite. You realise that if you charge Gunnersbury, my opposite number on the distaff side, Lieutenant Preece, will have to nobble Private Stopham. After all she was involved, too.'

'I couldn't help noticing that, sir.'

'I'll have to speak to Lieutenant Preece about it, then.'

'Thank you, sir. Bad for discipline.'

'And let you know our decision.'

'I'm sure it will be the right one, sir.'

Captain Pomona wasn't at all sure about that. Speaking to the pneumatic Lieutenant Preece about anything at all could prove very bad for his own discipline.

'And then, sir,' the CSM continued relentlessly, 'there's this civilian person studying birds on Horn.'

'Miss Joanna Bromley?'

'No, sir. I understand she confines her bird-watching to Hummel.' Hummel was an uninhabited rocky islet a quarter of a mile south of Horn and separated from it by a fierce tidal race.

'Tits,' said Captain Pomona, prompted by some awful Freudian urge. Joanna Bromley's upperworks were justly celebrated.

'Gannets,' said the CSM frostily. 'She's studying gannets. He was still smarting under Pomona's refusal to charge Corporal Gunnersbury and Private Stopham.

'It's the male bird person, sir. I believe he wishes to give the unit a lecture, sir.'

'You mean Dr Mathews. Yes, I asked him to. Good to get the boys and girls interested in something outside their work.'

'No trouble about that, sir.'

'I mean interested in something *else*, CSM.'

'Quite so, sir. Might I enquire the title of Dr Mathews's little talk, sir, so that I can get Mavis, I mean the orderly room clerk, to post it on Part Two Orders?'

Captain Pomona took a deep breath. 'I'm told he wants to call it: "The Mating habits of the Blackcock".'

Oh God, was there no escape?

CSM Markham saluted and made an about-turn so regimental that it left little doubt what he thought of the disciplinary standards of commissioned specialist technicians with dubious foreign-sounding names. After the echoes of the CSM's exit had died away, Captain Pomona sat staring at the unit strength chart on his office wall as if it might clarify his thoughts. Sadly, it had precisely the opposite effect. To Captain Pomona there seemed to be lines of sexuality connecting the individual names in a positive cat's-cradle of intrigue.

CSM Markham . . . Corporal Gunnersbury . . . Lance-Corporal Mason . . . He knew too well what they were up to with, respectively: radar tracker Cecilia Munt, a tall, thin girl with teeth like a horse; radar tracker Stopham and his orderly room clerk Mavis Prendergast.

Next came the two cooks, Privates Cassidy and Bond. His recent experience had given full meaning to the nickname 'Butch'.

Captain Pomona was a broad-minded man. He didn't necessarily disapprove of any of this. What troubled him was that sex in one form or another appeared to be undermining the efficiency of his command. A Russian rocket might easily sneak by while they were all at it. And this was something he was not prepared to condone.

The names of the Scots contingent cheered him slightly. There they were listed, men in one column, women in the other, poised as if to take part in their own eightsome reel.

It was the single name beneath his own that troubled him most of all – Lieutenant Regina Whymper, RAMC.

For reasons best known to itself, the Psychological Selection Department of the MOD had decided that its small specialised force on Horn needed a woman MO. The computer, or whatever kind of inspired guesswork the

MOD used, had come up with the name of Regina Whymper. Dr Whymper made Pomona think of Wagner in general and the Valkyries in particular. She was pushing forty and would, Captain Pomona had little doubt, have very much appreciated it if he would only start pushing her. He had no intention of complying. Being alone with Dr Whymper was like being corralled with a herd of amorous Aberdeen Angus heifers.

Nevertheless, she was the only medical authority he could turn to. His recent interview with CSM Markham had left him in little doubt that what he needed now was some sound medical advice about the over-heated state of his troops.

Pomona knocked on the MO's door. 'Enter,' throbbed the well-known contralto. Pomona stuck his head round the door and, seeing Dr Whymper was alone, prepared to withdraw it.

'Bertram!'

Pomona braced himself. Most people called him Bert.

'Bertram, you're not well. You don't *look* well.'

Already she was round the table and bearing down on him. He thought he knew in that instant what it must feel like to see an avalanche coming and to realise that you'd left your skis at home. Her hand was on his wrist, guiding him, no, towing him towards a chair. 'Open wide,' she said. Already the thermometer was flicking in the air.

Any protest he might have made was cut off as the mercury slid under his tongue. Her right hand seized his wrist and her index finger slid over the pressure point. The rest of the hand squeezed with more than practitioner's zeal as she felt his pulse rate.

Pomona managed to blurt round the thermometer: 'There's nothing the bloody matter with me.'

Dr Whymper sealed his lips over the glass tube with firm but loving fingers. 'We'll soon see about *that*.' She consulted the thermometer. 'Normal,' she declared.

'It's about the only damn thing around here that is.'

'Pulse rate up a little.' She heaved her considerable khaki bosom under his nose so that he caught the full strength of the cigarette smoke imbued in the barathea. 'Though perhaps,' she cooed with terrible coyness, 'we mustn't be entirely surprised about that.'

Captain Pomona rallied his forces. Was he or was he not in command here? 'I didn't come to see you about me.'

'You know you can speak freely to me about whatever it is that's troubling you. What is it?' she coaxed.

Captain Pomona plunged desperately. 'Sex,' he said.

'Bertram!' She was advancing most unprofessionally.

'Oh God,' he thought, 'what have I done now?'

'You can confide completely in me. I'm your doctor, you know.'

'Oh Christ,' Pomona thought. 'She probably believes I've got a dose of clap, though God knows where from.'

'You mustn't be shy.'

'I don't intend to be, Regina. I want to know if there's something you can put in the tea.'

Dr Whymper still obviously imagined that the problem was, exclusively, Pomona's.

'I'm sure we can find a better way of containing these entirely natural feelings than that.'

Pomona tried again. 'In prison they use bromide to calm the chaps, and I suppose the girls, down.'

'You wouldn't *like* bromide.'

Captain Pomona's patience was exhausted. If this went on, he'd need more than bromide.

'Regina, just listen to me for a second. It's not me. Well, not me, particularly. It's the whole bloody unit. It's as if being shut up here on this damned island with its unfortunate name does something to everyone. They can't think of anything else.'

'I think you're worrying too much,' she said. 'The pressures of command. I'll give you a mild sedative. Not that,' she said, twinkling with all the subtlety of a lighthouse, 'it will make any difference to you know what. And Bertram, if I may give a word of advice, let natural instincts have their outlet. I'll see we're, I mean they're, all on the pill. After that, give the troops plenty of outside interests, bird-watching, climbing, botany, stags, seals, the wonders of the natural world. They're all here on Horn. We could form a natural history society. Interests are better than half a ton of bromide in the tea. Besides, they'd spot it.'

Pomona's mind reeled as he listened to the MO trotting out the standard service recipe. Well, maybe there was a grain of sense in it all, but he doubted whether the birds and the bees were the right subjects for study. There was at least this to be said for them: they did get it all over in one season. For a moment Captain Bertram Pomona envied them.

'Have a word with the NERTS,' Dr Whymper suggested brightly.

In the backroom of the cottage that served NERTS as a laboratory, Graham MacCallister, aged twenty-three, six-foot-one, red-haired and good-looking, was moodily dissecting a deer dropping.

The correct abbreviation was N.E.R.T. It stood for National Environmental Research Trust. Not surprisingly, the Trust and all who worked for it were known as 'NERTS' or 'THE NERTS'.

Horn had been uninhabited since the outbreak of the First World War until the Army decided to set up a radar station there.

NERTS had come to Horn a year after the Army, primarily to study its isolated red deer herd but also its bird life, notably blackcock and gannets. The NERTS occupied a huddle of renovated crofters' cottages, half a mile from the tracking unit and situated beside Horn's diminutive harbour. There they were ministered to by two islanders, MacGregor, a former shepherd and now general man about the hill, and Flora Flodden, their housekeeper. The NERTS project consisted of two female and four male scientists of whom Graham MacCallister was one. His role in the red deer project was the study of faecal pellets.

Despite a good First in Zoology, Graham sometimes wondered whether he was cut out for a scientific career. He doubted whether he had either the dedication or the scientific detachment.

The mere phrase 'scientific detachment' made him think of the lovely Dr Janet Morgan. Now there *was* an advanced case of scientific detachment. Graham had no doubt that he was deeply infatuated, if not deeply in love, with the raven-haired, green-eyed Dr Morgan. As for Dr Morgan! *Oestrus* was about the most romantic word in her vocabulary. The sexual receptiveness, or otherwise, of a red deer hind, was the nearest she appeared to get to thoughts of love.

As Graham teased open another deer dropping, separating the strands of half-digested bog cotton from the matted fibres of poor quality heather, his hand shook. Graham had no doubt what was making his fingers tremble. It was the thought of Janet, only next door, in the darkroom, alone. What an opportunity for any red-blooded young man. He toyed with the idea of charging next door and throwing his arms around her. Fortunately, he controlled himself. Janet had scientific detachment up to her lovely eyebrows. She would merely have assumed that he had come to look at her contact prints.

He enclosed the dissected pellet in a plastic bag and wrote on the label: 'Collected at 500 feet, Ben Dhui.' Given the fact that a red deer's digestive system took six hours to process raw vegetation into faecal matter, this meant that the deer had moved from the 2000 foot level, where the poorish heather grew, to the point at which it had defecated, within six hours. Fascinating! He wondered what the hell posterity would do with this useless piece of information.

Graham looked up as Janet entered softly from the darkroom. His initial pleasure turned to pain as he saw that Dr Hammond Hulke was following her, as it were, nose to tail.

Janet was holding a sheet of still-wet contact prints, the result of her previous day's hind stalking. Each shot, made with a 300 mm lens, showed a close-up of a female deer's hind quarters with the sexual organs as the centre of the target. Hulke's six-foot-two of solid brawn moved in a perpetual forward stoop. This attitude reminded Graham of a stag pursuing a hind to sniff, or as Janet would say, sexually sample her. Graham's only consolation was that Janet Morgan looked unsampled, not to say unsniffed.

If anything she looked sniffy at being even remotely sampled.

Janet acknowledged Graham's presence with: 'Anything new in the faeces today?'

'Some low grade heather in a pellet collected at five hundred feet.'

'Interesting.'

'Janet's got some fantastic close-ups of vaginas,' Hulke said coarsely.

'Anything showing?' Graham felt he had to display interest.

Hulke clapped him on the back. 'Everything my dear boy. But *everything*. Maybe we could sell them to *Stag*.' *Stag* was one of the girlie mags he had sent over from the mainland seventy-five miles away on the fortnightly supply trawler SS *Haddie*.

'I meant any signs of *oestrus*.'

'I'm not sure. Look at this fifth shot,' Janet invited eagerly. 'Of course, it's early days yet, but there do seem to be possible signs of inflammation there.'

'Wow!' said Hulke.

Graham said irritably. 'Why don't you go and find a nice crag to roar from, Hammond?'

Hulke's study was the rutting pattern of Horn's stags. Hulke obligingly climbed on to a chair and began to give a life-like imitation of a stag roaring. Next, Hulke lifted the chair in front of him and lowered his head as if to charge a rival male with his antlers. 'I think,' he said, 'since the gorgeous Dr Morgan isn't yet ready to answer my rutting roar, I'll retire to my private corrie and rub off the remains of my velvet on a large gin and tonic.'

When Hulke had gone, Graham said: 'Don't you find Hammond rather tedious?'

'I can't say I notice him much.'

'I mean he's always trying it on.'

'Trying it on?'

'With you.'

'Oh, *that*!'

'Doesn't it worry you?'

'No. It's only what I expect from him.'

'Fergus Roxborough tries it on, too.' Dr Fergus Roxborough was head of the project.

'Does he?'

'You know he does, only he's much smoother with it.'

Janet turned to face him. Her eyes below those two raven's wings of soft hair were an amazing green like the deep onyx water beneath the cliffs of Hummel.

'And you, Graham, I suppose you'd never try it on, as you so unscientifically phrase it.'

'I wouldn't try it on in the same way.'

'But you'd like to.' It was a statement of fact, or maybe a research worker's enquiry. There was not a hint of coquetry, let alone encouragement, in it.

'Janet, I think you're lovely. Can't we forget all this scientific gobbledegook and go for a walk sometimes?'

'To try it on?' The green eyes were interested rather than amused.

'No. Not like that, anyway. Not unless you wished it.' Graham felt himself blushing. He hadn't meant to say anything like that.

'Please don't be embarrassed, Graham. Everything you, Hammond and Fergus feel is only to be expected. Looked at from a scientific point of view you are conforming to the normal courtship pattern of an isolated bachelor herd. It doesn't worry me, or for that matter flatter me, in the very least.'

'Oh shit!' said Graham and flung his last pellet sample out of the window.

Dr Jerry Mathews was having no such trouble with Joanna Bromley.

'Come and see my lek,' he had invited not for the first time. The lekking ground where the blackcock males displayed to their hens in early springtime lay in a sheltered dell half a mile from the cottages on a sunny slope beneath a silver birch plantation.

Joanna needed no second invitation. It was a place little visited by either the deer unit or the army. To reach it meant clambering over a disordered pile of granite boulders. This, despite her generous build, was nothing to a girl whose Ph.D. depended on regularly scaling the heights of the islet of Hummel to study the mating rituals of nesting gannets.

They were playing a favourite game, Jerry scampering about in a stooping posture fluttering his arms in a crazy imitation of a displaying blackcock, Joanna coyly darting away like a well-wooed greyhen. Every now and again Jerry would somehow manage to flutter off a garment shortly to be followed by an answering action from Joanna.

When they were naked, the game changed. Plucking a wildflower and holding it in her mouth, Joanna came swooping in with arms outstretched in a fair imitation of a gannet, presenting its mate with nesting material. The posture accentuated the full splendour of the girl's bosom.

'I see now why they call gannets boobies.'

'Shut up and accept my gift.'

She forced the flower into Jerry's mouth and they kissed, laughing.

'Booby.'

'Don't be personal or I shan't bring you any more nesting material.'

'I didn't think female gannets did that.'

'I'm a hen's libber.'

'It won't do you any good. Gannets won't mate with blackcock. It's probably something to do with the Race Relations Act. Any member of the British Trust for Ornithology knows that.'

'Not this one.'

A few seconds later, he said: 'Hey, gannets aren't supposed to do things like that.'

And several minutes later, she said: 'I never really see how birds get much fun out of it.'

'Or bees.'

'Particularly bees. They do it with flowers.'

'Darling, isn't lek a lovely word? So much prettier. You're a lovely lekker.'

Some five minutes later, she said: 'I've often felt sorry for gannets.'

'Me, too, for blackcocks.'

'Darling, wouldn't it be awful if we were like birds and only felt like this a few weeks every year.'

Dr Fergus Roxborough, head of NERTS on Horn, was forty-five. He had iron-grey hair which crinkled as if made of pressed steel, and looked metallic enough to jangle when he brushed it. Its apparent tensile strength suggested it might break the teeth of a comb. Early on in his career he had made a name for himself with a monograph on the breeding biology of stoats. There were those among his colleagues, rival NERTS especially, who said that everything or anyone he had subsequently done had been a natural sequel to that work. A scientific enemy had once described Fergus Roxborough as suffering from an advanced attack of Neat Face. His features were well ordered and well pointed. His grey rectangular moustache might have been regularly trimmed by a topiarist. The result suggested the business end of a miniature bass broom suspended between upper lip and nose. To be fair, which no one in Dr Fergus Roxborough's circle ever liked to be, he was not a bad scientist. He was successful, successful in the field and successful in the all-important lobbies and committees which got people interesting jobs. He was also, or so he told himself and other people, consistently successful with women. Roxborough's conceit was enormous. One day, he assured himself, his charm would even prove too much for Dr Janet Morgan.

Roxborough's field telephone rang.

'Bert Pomona here.'

'Hello, Captain. Roxborough speaking.'

'On the MO's advice, I'm arranging a recreational and educational programme for my boys and girls. I'm wondering if you'd give them a talk on deer and that kind of thing.'

'What kind of thing?' Roxborough's tidy mind was puzzled.

'What they get up to. I mean what you people are studying.'

'Broadly speaking we're concerned with breeding successes, reproduction, mating behaviour.'

Roxborough thought he heard a groan at the other end of the line.

'Did you get that, Captain Pomona?'

'Yes, thanks. I was hoping there might be a different line you could take, something perhaps more neutral. More suitable for a mixed unit. Monarch of the Glen and all that.'

'I can't think of anything less likely to inspire an outbreak of looting and rape among the common soldiery than the reproductive behaviour of *Cervus elephas*. I mean they're so unlike us in every way.'

'That's a relief, then.'

The line gave a clunk and went dead.

At that moment MacGregor was wheeling his ancient Greaves scrambler motorcycle out of the outhouse at the back of the NERTS cottages. After watching an exhibition of rough-riding at a Highland gathering, he had decided that the acquisition of a cross-country Greaves would aid him in his work as a shepherd. With a little practice, he had felt certain, he would be able to roar around the hill, jumping burns and boulders just as the exhibition riders had done. Within a few weeks, MacGregor's sheep would willingly have put up with all the chivvying collies in the kingdom in exchange for silencing for ever the snarl of the Greaves' 350 cc Anzani engine. Relief for his flocks had come with the arrival on the island of the NERTS. Dr Roxborough had rapidly co-opted MacGregor as part-time ghillie and general man-about-the-hill. Equally rapidly he had banned the use of the Greaves. Henceforward, there would be no more scrambling. Nothing was to be allowed to disturb the pristine peace of Horn's red deer herds.

Dr Roxborough had confined MacGregor's motorbike to Horn's two tracks, the one between the cottages and the Radar Tracking Unit and the even rougher route that connected MacGregor's cottage with his shearing shed halfway up Horn's highest mountain, the 3000 ft Ben Dhui. MacGregor regretted the banning of the Greaves, but the salary paid to him by NERTS more than compensated for the deprivation. The scrambler had only one more role to play in his life. It had, he had discovered, a remarkable effect on Flora Flodden. Flora had accompanied NERTS from the mainland to act as cook and housekeeper. MacGregor had fancied the thirty-ish, no-nonsense Flora at first sight but had found her as unresponsive as a granite boulder. He had long reluctantly dismissed her as a 'yeld', or barren hind. But for some reason he could not understand she lusted after a ride on his pillion. MacGregor had once persuaded her to hoist her tartaned rump on to a cushion strapped on behind his saddle. Then, roaring and jouncing, snarling and slithering, enveloped in an intoxicating reek of burning castor oil, he had borne her up the track to his shearing shed. Flora had arrived all shook up. The rhythm of that wild ride had somehow got to her. Just as the Sabine women had been softened up by a quick cross-country gallop, so had something been stirred deep in fortress Flora. The drawbridge had almost come down. MacGregor had even persuaded her to enter his shearing shed, to recline on the conveniently arranged fleeces therein. He might even have reached that other more personal fleece had not one of MacGregor's rams decided to charge the door at that precise moment.

MacGregor, who was close to his sheep, later wondered if the ram had been motivated by jealousy. The interruption had been enough. Flora had, as it were, re-posted sentries and dropped the portcullis. Fortress Flora remained impregnable, contrary to later rumours encouraged by MacGregor himself.

Flora had been silent on the even wilder ride back. She had remained frosty as the north face of Ben Dhui ever since. Nevertheless MacGregor was certain that he now knew her weakness. He had observed her several times sneaking round the back of his cottage to take secret looks at the Greaves. He had even watched her stroking its saddle. He had little doubt that one day soon she would again succumb to its tempestuous magic. This time he would make sure that damn ram was a mile or two away on the hill.

He wheeled the gaunt machine on to the knoll behind the cottages and propped it up on its stand. With an oily rag he began sensuously to caress its shining silver crankcase. He turned the wheel head-on towards Flora's cottage. The curiously upward-raked handlebars with their dependant brake and clutch levers resembled the antlers and brow tines of an eager stag. To heighten the illusion he thrust down on the kickstart and gunned the engine. The aphrodisiac odour of Castrol R floated on the evening breeze towards Flora Flodden's outwardly unreceptive nostrils.

Early September

Captain Pomona's door flew open as if it had been leant on by an overdose of plastic explosive. Dr Whymper stood there.

'Bertram. Isn't it wonderful. The whole unit wants to attend our two little talks. So much for "E" for Education. Now what we need is some "R" for Recreation. I've been speaking to MacGregor about it.'

'About what?'

'About the dancing.'

'What dancing, for God's sake?'

'Highland dancing.'

'First I've heard of it.'

'Silly! It's the recreational part of our programme. MacGregor can do it.'

'I don't doubt it. Everyone on this damned island can do it.'

'Play the music, I mean. He's got his pipes at the cottage.'

Pomona shuddered. If there was one thing he could do without in the Highland scene it was the bagpipes.

'I should settle for the record player. More dependable.'

'And he knows all the movements.'

Pomona's fevered mind immediately pictured the interior of the shearing shed.

'The "Eightsome" . . .'

'Twosomes are quite enough.'

'And, of course, the "Strathspey", the "Dashing White Sergeant" and "Strip the Willow". And as a bit of fun, there's the "Gay Gordons".'

Pomona's thoughts for some reason flew to the cookhouse. Still, even that would be a relief after the implications of 'Strip the Willow'.

Regina Whymper lowered her vast barathea backside on to the corner, or rather one half of his desk. It reminded him of a landslide on a mountain built exclusively of khaki mousse. He caught the familiar tang of cigarette smoke mixed with *Je Reviens* in proportion of four to one.

'So you see, Bertram, we can begin on Scottish dancing classes straight away.'

'Are you sure they're the right thing?'

'Of course, every bit as fit-making at PT and a good deal more exciting.'

Pomona agreed about the last bit. To tell the truth, he had always found Scottish dancing rather erotic. The girls looked so prim. Like naughty governesses. Those black shoes. The pointed toes. The bosom-accentuating lace at the throat. Or was he getting mixed up? Wasn't that the men? God knows *their* dress was provocative enough. The jiggling sporrans like demented pubic hair. The dirks! Like a lot of bloody turkey cocks.

'Perhaps we could just confine it to the military ones. Like the sword dance.' Even he couldn't see sexual overtones in hopping around a couple of rusty bayonets drawn from the stores.

'Most Scottish dances have a military origin, Bertram. In a Highland regiment, the Pipe-Major makes the subalterns parade for a dancing class every day before breakfast.'

'I can't see it working here, Regina. I mean there's only one subaltern, Lieutenant Preece.'

The MO veered quickly away from the subject of Lieutenant Preece.

'Of course not, Bertram. That's why we're going to do it differently. Classes will be held twice a week in recreational periods. I shall take them myself.'

'I doubt if you'll get many volunteers.'

'That's why I want you to make classes a parade, as in a proper Highland regiment.'

'I doubt if it will be very popular.'

'Popularity is not necessarily something to be sought by a commanding officer, Bertram.'

'I'm quite aware of the responsibilities of command.'

'Of course you are, dear boy. So I know you'd be the first to offer my Scottish dancers a little incentive.'

'Such as what? A free issue of black pudden?'

'Naughty Captain Pomona. No! After a week or two of

classes we're going to reward the unit with a dance. We'll invite the NERTS, too. It will be a marvellous way of getting everyone together.'

Captain Pomona loved his job but now he seriously wondered if it wasn't time to put in for a posting.

Dr Jerry Mathews had decided that it was such fun pretending to be a blackcock to Joanna's coyly co-operative greyhen that he would enliven his lecture to Captain Pomona's boys and girls by actually holding it on the lekking ground. The idea had come to him one afternoon when, on a cushion of fragrantly pliant heather, his lek with Joanna had come to its predictable and delightful conclusion.

'They'll enjoy it so much more with a practical demonstration.'

'I don't doubt it, Jerry; you're awfully heavy and this heather *is* rather prickly.'

'Greyhens never complain.'

'Blackcocks don't weigh twelve stone in their walking boots. Besides they tread the hens.'

'Kinky, even without walking boots.'

'Do you know, before I took my degree, I never knew how birds actually did it.'

'Very brief business, treading.'

'Much more fun lekking.'

'I *like* lekking.'

'Come on, let's lek,' he said, nibbling her ear.

'Jerry, that's not real lekking. You're supposed to rush about displaying to me.'

'No. We've done that bit. Lekking is just to get to know each other. I feel I've known you all my life.'

'Very unornithological,' she said; and a few minutes later with a deep sigh: 'Who'd ever want to be a bird?'

As they were dressing he said: 'Yes. I've definitely decided. I'll give my lecture out here. They can act out the lek . . . or anyway the first part of it.'

For a compulsory parade the turn-out for Scottish dancing instruction was not bad. Dr Whymper formed up her

Eightsome with a manner somewhere between that of a female concentration camp guard and a Girl Guide mistress.

'The CSM opposite Private Munt. Then Corporal Gunnersbury and Private Stopham. The cooks next. Now let me see. Who else have we? No, not you Captain Pomona. I'll use you for demonstration purposes.'

Pomona felt his eyes going out of focus.

'Yes, that leaves Private Prendergast and Lance-Corporal Mason. I think that's very nice pairing.'

Too bloody nice, thought Pomona.

The MO boomed on: 'Of course, as the dance progresses, you'll all get mixed up.'

That, too, seemed possible.

The door opened to admit Lieutenant Myfanwy Preece. Pomona noticed with approval that she wore a tartan mini skirt.

'Ooh, sorry, Doc,' she said, 'I only just got off watch.'

'You shouldn't have bothered to change,' Dr Whymper said in a forty-degrees-below-zero voice. She addressed the dancers. 'Just for the record, this instructional class is a parade. Dress will be PT gear in future.'

Lance-Corporal Mason tore his eyes away from Myfanwy Preece's shimmering lower limbs and said out of the side of his mouth to Corporal Gunnersbury. 'I don't see how you could get much more PT than that.'

Dr Whymper glanced at Bertram Pomona. His eyes, likewise, fixed to Lieutenant Preece's creamy thighs, stood out like cairngorms on the hilt of an ornamental Sgiandubh. With daggers, or perhaps dirks, in her own eyes, the MO said in her most menacing vibrato: 'Now, *Sir*, if I could have your attention, please.'

'What would you like me to do?' Myfanwy Preece asked prettily.

Dr Whymper fought to control herself from making a positive suggestion.

'Perhaps you could use the Lieutenant to demonstrate with me?' Pomona suggested hopefully.

'*I* shall demonstrate with you, sir. One of us has to know the moves.'

A fleetingly reminiscent smile passed over Pomona's face.

Dr Whymper put the pick-up arm down on the record player and that first shattering chord that announces that the orchestra is about to declare musical war on all Sassenachs reverberated from the walls of the equipment store. Then Jimmy Shand launched his attack with bagpipes in the van and the rest of the instruments bounding forward, regardless of death or defeat, like the clans at Culloden.

'Scottish dancing,' Dr Whymper was saying, 'is obscure in its origins.'

Pomona thought to himself. 'I'll bet the old bag got it all out of books.'

'Some people say . . .' Dr Whymper's rich contralto was more than a match for the combined forces of Jimmy Shand . . . 'That it goes back to the Druids, in which case much of it probably derives from early fertility rites.'

Corporal Gunnersbury caught the eye of Private Gwladys 'Drop 'em' Stopham. He grinned and whispered: 'Go easy on the fertility bit, love.'

'Most of you . . .' Dr Whymper went on, 'will have noticed how in Scottish dancing the men hold both arms raised above their heads. Go on, all you men. I want you to do that now.'

Self-consciously, Pomona and the other four males raised their hands in the air.

'Now, Private Prendergast. What do they remind you of?'

Mavis said doubtfully. 'Are they surrendering?'

'Surrendering?' thundered the MO. 'Of course they're not surrendering. They're dominating.'

'Oh, I see.' Mavis who was obviously rather intrigued by this thought smiled provocatively at Lance-Corporal Mason.

'Lieutenant Preece. What do you imagine they're saying to us?'

Mason had lowered one arm to squeeze Mavis's elbow.

'For a start, Lance-Corporal Mason looks as though he wants to leave the room.'

She got her laugh. *All square,* she thought.

Dr Whymper laughed too, but with a hint of death rattle in it.

'Corporal, put up your other arm please before you inspire any more little jokes. Now all of you men, dance round in a circle with your arms raised. Can't you see now, ladies? They're imitating stags and you are the females they're competing for.'

Pomona groaned. He'd known all along the way things were bound to go.

Jimmy Shand crashed to a halt.

'Now, first of all,' Dr Whymper was saying, 'we'll all learn the *Pas de Basque* or travelling step.'

Watch-keeping tended to fall into two sections, one composed of the English element of the unit, the other made up by the Scottish. It was the Scottish detail who clicked for Jerry Mathews's lekking lecture and on-site demonstration of blackcock mating rituals.

Jerry Mathews had picked a lovely afternoon for his lekking demonstration. The parade mustered under Corporal Dunfee, a soft-spoken and outwardly restrained Aberdonian with the build and Chippendale legs of a Jack Russell terrier.

The eight Scots had started out from the small parade ground at what passed in the Radar Tracking Unit for a smart military pace. The uneven nature of the terrain soon prompted Corporal Dunfee to order his party, somewhat too late to catch up with circumstances, to break step. The effect of this order had been to convert the march into something more closely resembling a lover's stroll or perhaps a nature ramble. On receiving the order originally designed by the military mind to protect unwary bridges from being pulverised by the stamp of well-drilled feet descending in unison, the parade sorted itself out according to individual affinities, at least half the pairs so formed proceeding from that point onwards hand-in-hand.

By the time they reached the lekking ground, the parade was hot if not especially bothered. The lecturer had wisely provided for this eventuality by depositing earlier in the day a crate of canned beer in a shady place. So now, beer in hand, the class sat around on convenient granite boulders or lolled luxuriously on the tufty grass while Jerry began his exposition.

Jerry had a natural and colloquially pleasing style. He began by handing round blown-up stills of a magnificently randy blackcock with white tail fanned out.

'Notice,' he said, 'the white frills curiously reminiscent of the lace jabot at the throat of the Highland dandy but in the case of the blackcock, worn at the other end.'

'What do the lassies wear?' Private Jeannie McCall demanded. A short well-upholstered brunette from Glasgow, Jeannie voted Scottish Nationalist and was known to be incensed by the fact that the British Army had never yet appointed a woman Field-Marshal, and showed little sign of intending to change its policy.

Jerry told her: 'I'm afraid they're rather drab. In fact they're called greyhens for obvious reasons.'

'Typical,' Jeannie said. 'I'll bet the whole bluidy system was invented by a man.'

Corporal Dunfee who had held Jeannie McCall's hand during the long march to the lekking ground grinned. 'And why not, Jeannie. I've never heard you object to a little male dominance.'

'You're no' a blackcock, Corporal Dunfee.'

'Er, quite,' said Jerry who thought it better that this line of thought did not develop. 'The lek starts in March or April when the cocks begin to gather on the display ground.'

'What about the females?' Jeannie persisted.

'They come later.'

'Bluidy men!'

'First the males arrive in all their finery. They sort the ground out into territories. They sing with a sort of *rookooing* noise and early each morning dance round each other. Sometimes they do this for days on end.'

Jeannie wasn't to be placated. 'Vain bastards.'

'They also fight.'

'Like a Glasgae' pub on a Saturday night.'

The rest of the class was now enjoying Jeannie's contrapuntal commentary. Jerry, seeing he had the attention of his lay audience, played up to her.

'Of course, the fights are really mostly sham. It's very seldom anyone gets hurt.'

'Bluidy cowards.'

'Except by accident.'

'My old man,' informed the bonnie Jeannie, 'got his head split open by a broken bottle – by accident.'

'At last the hens arrive on the scene.'

'About bluidy time, if you ask me. I'll bet the damn men take no notice of them.'

'Well, not at first,' agreed Jerry. 'But they puff themselves up and the red wattle above the eye stands erect.'

'No comment,' said Jeannie.

'Then they sort of stretch their necks and bow down.'

'We should be so lucky.'

'The funny thing is, it isn't always the most magnificent cock who scores with the ladies.'

'Anyone can understand that,' said Jeannie looking straight at Corporal Dunfee.

'Coition,' began Jerry.

'What was that again, doctor?'

'Coition . . . Copulation.'

'That's what I thought you said.'

'Often takes place here on the lekking ground. After that the hens just go off on their own, later to lay their eggs and rear their families.'

'And I suppose the bluidy cocks leave them to get on with it.'

'Yes, that's the way it works with blackcock.'

'And with quite a few white cocks,' said Jeannie.

Corporal Dunfee felt it was time he showed some intelligent interest to compensate for and, if possible, divert Jeannie.

'What's all the dancing in aid of?'

'It appears to be necessary to bring both males and females to breeding pitch.'

'Just like the Sergeants' mess,' Jeannie explained.

'Something like,' Jerry agreed, 'though that's hardly as colourful.'

'In that case, you haven't seen CSM Markham in full display,' Jeannie said.

'And, of course, the Sergeants mess use other equally powerful forms of stimulation.' Jerry held up his can of McEwan's strong ale. 'Now, when you've all drunk your beer, I'm going to make you give a practical demonstration. Joanna will place the men in typical blackcock territories. I'll demonstrate the actions of their dance and then we'll bring the hens into the picture.'

They took their places on the lekking ground. Guided by Joanna and Jerry they acted out the blackcock and greyhen courtship rituals, seriously at first but gradually they began to fall about with laughter.

The lecture and demonstration was voted to have been a great success. After it was over, the parade melted away into the heather, to put what they had learned into practice.

'Tonight at 1930 hrs. in the mess hut,' announced Part Two Orders. 'Everyone off duty will attend. A lecture entitled "Onset of the Rut" will be given by Dr Fergus Roxborough, "Monarch of the Glen".'

Captain Pomona had averted his eyes when he read this. He found it difficult to imagine how Private Prendergast could have arranged the announcement in precisely this disorder.

Roxborough, if not quite as noble as Landseer's famous stag, nevertheless struck an imposing figure as he three-quarter faced his audience, best profile carefully aligned.

'You have all heard,' he was saying, 'of a stag party. Possibly you have even taken part in one.'

An interior flash shot of the NCO mess was projected on to the screen. From it CSM Markham leered morbidly over a pint of bitter. Corporal Dunfee lugubriously sipped a brown ale. In the background, Corporal Gunnersbury and Lance-Corporal Mason played cribbage on a beer-stained table littered with empty pint glasses.

The audience cheered and booed. The boos led by Private Stopham were mainly for CSM Markham.

'Notice there are no women present,' Roxborough said.

More boos than cheers this time.

'This is exactly the way the red deer stags behave for much of the time between Spring and the rutting season in September and October. Hence the term "stag party".'

'What about the lassies?' demanded Jeannie McCall.

'They go around together, too, usually under the sharp eye of an old female.'

A picture appeared on the screen of an alert hind, head raised, ears cocked, looking towards camera with ten or so lesser hinds scattered across the heather background.

'She's got a frustrated look, just like old Regina,' Private Stopham's whisper was loud enough to make the old hind in question bark sharply. The MO tried to turn her snort of disapproval into a cigarette cough.

'In human terms there are disadvantages to the system of segregating the sexes,' Dr Roxborough continued.

'I'll say,' Corporal Gunnersbury muttered.

'Butch' Cassidy and the hideous Doris '007' Bond exchanged a glance that would have burned the porridge for which the latter was so justly feared.

'On the other hand, there are compensations. Until the onset of the rut, both males and females live amicably together and without sexual complications. Then, around the end of September, the picture changes.'

Dr Roxborough switched on a tape recorder. A hoarse roaring filled the room. It had a rasping quality, which spoke of raw, damp places and sore throats, far beyond the range of the human larynx to produce.

A succession of slides followed showing a Master stag seeing off a rival; two stags locked antler to antler in battle, while a third and decidedly inferior beast made off with a couple of wayward females. A big stag copulating drew a brief, sympathetic cheer from the audience.

'Alas,' said Dr Roxborough sadly, 'It's all over in seconds and the poor chap has to serve as many as ten or twenty hinds as well as fighting off younger and perhaps fitter rivals.'

'I'd never last,' observed Corporal Dunfee.

A further slide showed the big stag literally on his knees.

In fact he had got down like this to decorate his antlers with mud but Dr Roxborough saw no reason to spoil the fun.

'And what happens when the rut is over?' Dr Roxborough asked rhetorically. 'Why, the stags forget the whole business of sex for another eleven months. All they have to do now is to feed themselves through the winter in order to grow a new and more magnificent set of antlers in the Spring. And the purpose of those antlers? As far as we know, largely to impress other stags and win more females . . . in fact to become the monarch of the glen . . . by the onset of the rut.'

Dr Roxborough congratulated himself that he had extremely neatly rounded things off with the title and subtitle of his lecture.

There was an enthusiastic spatter of clapping, enlivened by Lance-Corporal Mason's impression of a stag roaring.

'I'll be delighted to answer any questions.'

Dr Whymper felt it was up to her to lead off with something vaguely medical and intelligent.

'How long are the hinds in a state of *oestrus*?'

'Only for a matter of days.'

'Do you mean on heat?' CSM asked. He liked to get that sort of thing straight.

'Precisely.'

'Only three or four days out of three hundred and sixty-five?' Private Stopham was considerably impressed.

'On the average. Yes.'

'Do you mean,' Private Stopham persisted, 'that the poor creatures' sex lives last under a week all told.'

'You could say that.'

There was a shocked silence while the Radar Tracking Unit digested this incredible fact.

Captain Pomona felt it was time that he weighed in.

'I must say that it does seem to me that it must be quite beneficial to be able to, well, get on with things for the rest of the year without being troubled by . . . well, you know what I mean . . . without sex,' he burbled desperately, hoping the message was getting home to his troops, 'getting in the way of one's work and all that kind of thing.'

Another shocked silence followed this heresy. Private McCall predictably broke it.

'Aye, it's great for you but what about the puir lassies. They'll all be in the club, no doubt.'

'Getting the hinds pregnant is, after all, the entire object of having a rutting season,' Roxborough reminded Private McCall sharply.

'They don't have the pill, Jeannie dear,' Mavis Prendergast explained.

'Well,' said Jeannie, 'the only advantage I can see in the whole damn stupid system is that they don't have the Curse either.'

Question time had now entered a gynaecological minefield into which the girls and even Dr Whymper were plainly only too ready to dash.

Captain Pomona rose to wind up the occasion just as Dr Whymper was saying: 'One can see how exciting it must be to have only the most handsome and strongest males competing for one's favours . . .'

Captain Pomona rose to thank the speaker. 'Ladies and gentlemen,' he began; *Jesus Christ!* he thought.

Late September

'I suppose,' Hammond Hulke said, 'I'll have to put in an appearance at this bloody dance of theirs.'

Graham watched Hulke swill back a large Glenlivet. There had been enough in the last bottle of malt for a single apiece. Now the NERTS mess would have to wait until the fortnightly supply ship *Haddie* called again. Typically, the horrible Hulke had not offered to share the whisky.

'Don't forget to sign the book for a large one,' Graham told him. It was nothing unusual for Hulke to forget to sign the book altogether.

Hulke grinned evilly. 'You going to the dance?'

'I hadn't thought of it.'

'You mean you *had* thought of it, but the lovely Dr Morgan has turned you down.'

'You should know, Hulke.'

'I do. She turned me down, too. Likewise our beloved leader.'

'So neither you nor Fergus are going?'

'Not at all. Fergus feels he has to attend as head of mission. Me, I shall just go for the booze. The first round is on the Army apparently.'

'I bet you do better than that.'

Hulke winked and held up his empty glass. 'Cheers! You never know, there may be a bit of Army crumpet going begging. They tell me they're a hot lot. It's a full moon, by the way.'

Graham said loftily: 'In that case I may go out on the hill. I've always wanted to climb Ben Dhui at night.'

'Excellent! Nothing like a spot of exercise. Better than a cold shower. Get all those lascivious thoughts out of your young head.'

This was not precisely what Graham had in mind. He found Janet preserving the uterus of a barren hind that Hulke had shot the previous day.

'Definite traces of hermaphroditism,' Janet said without looking up.

'Since neither of us are going to the Army's dance, I've got a suggestion to make.'

'Oh, yes.' Janet transferred a long dangling red gobbet of membrane to a test tube of formaldehyde.

'It's a full moon that night.'

'What's that got to do with anything?'

'I rather thought I'd go out on the hill. I've always wanted to see the island from Ben Dhui at night.'

'Stags are likely to be very active,' she said.

Graham hadn't thought of the climb in connection with his work.

Janet was interested now. 'And the hinds, too. We'll be well into the start of the rut by then.'

'Exactly. So I thought perhaps we might make the climb together.'

Janet laid her grave green eyes firmly but gently on him so that his heart leapt like a sea trout in the burn.

'Oh no,' she said. 'That wouldn't do at all. We'd see *so* much more if we observed separately. Besides we'd be less likely to disturb them. We might even discover how much copulation goes on at night.'

'I doubt it,' Graham said with feeling.

Outside he met MacGregor. It was hard to miss him. He was sitting outside Flora Flodden's kitchen window on the saddle of the parked Greaves playing a forlorn love-lilt on the bagpipes. So far his only reward had been that Flora had twice appeared at an upstairs window and shaken a carpet at him.

Graham waited until the chant, haunting and wild as a curlew's song, had died. Knowing the depth of MacGregor's passion and, in his present unrequited state, deeply sympathising, he said: 'If she resists that she must have a heart of stone.'

'Aye, of granite, Graham. And yourself?'

MacGregor was a keen observer of nature and his observations were by no means confined to the behaviour of deer and ptarmigan, black grouse and buzzard.

'Like granite, too. I'm afraid.'

MacGregor sighed. He gestured with the pipes in the direction of Flora's cottage.

'I was hoping to persuade yon auld yeld to come to the sojers' dance.'

'Me, likewise.'

'The guid wee doctor Morgan?'

'Aye,' said Graham falling into the patois.

'She'll no accompany you?'

'Too bloody true. So I'm thinking of climbing Ben Dhui that night.'

'Aye, the full moon.'

'That's right.'

'And the stags rutting. How did *you* know about the magic?'

'What magic?'

'That it's the time for lovers to be climbing Ben Dhui.'

'I didn't.'

'It's an auld belief of the folk who once lived here. He who reaches the Tine of Horn at the top of Ben Dhui on the September moon and hears a great stag roaring nearby shall have his way with the lassie of his choice.'

'Does it work?'

'Highland and island folk do not invent such things.'

'Have you tried it MacGregor?'

'Aye, once long ago.'

'And what happened?'

'I'm no saying. But there's more to the legend than just temporary gratification of the senses. If you can persuade the lassie to join you there, then she'll be true to you, and you to her, for life.'

'But it didn't work in your case?'

'I'm a single man so you have your answer. But then I never persuaded the lassie to scale the Tine with me. Anyway, it was long ago.'

'Now you've a mind to try again.'

'Och, I've no wish to be true to Flora Flodden for the rest of my life but I'm no saying I'd forego the gratification of the senses.'

'You're on then. Provided we get a clear sky we'll climb it together.'

Captain Pomona privately thought that the idea of a dance among twenty odd people who saw each other daily and, in not a few cases, knew each other intimately, was the product of a deranged brain. He had carefully considered whether this view might not be part of the paranoia he was increasingly experiencing in connection with the behaviour of his unit in general and its operational efficiency in particular. On the whole he thought not. Since the brain concerned was that of the MO, Dr Regina Whymper, he decided that he had been right the first time. To hold a dance *was* crazy, especially when it was intended to be a Scottish dance, the terpsichorean expertise for which had been acquired by all concerned in some half-a-dozen lessons conducted by the MO herself. Captain Pomona reflected gloomily that he was expected to attend – for morale's sake, as Reggie Whymper had put it.

It was Captain Pomona's considered judgement that no one born south of the Great Glen, and certainly no Sassenach of remote Italian ancestry like himself, should be expected to dance the Eightsome, let alone the Strathspey, without access to a computer. While trying to follow Dr Whymper's instructions in class he had twice ended up facing the wall – a different wall on each occasion – instead of his partner and had once found himself dancing with CSM Markham instead of Dr Whymper.

So severely battered was he by everything the Scottish dance had done to him that he had weakly acceded to Reggie Whymper's final demand. As she had phrased it: 'Bertram, I do think you ought to let the boys and girls dance in civvies. The kilt is so much more atmospheric. Most of the Scottish contingent have their own kilts and it will add to the fun if the rest have to improvise. Sort of fancy dress.'

Bertram Pomona's mind did an all too familiar boggle at the thought of what CSM Markham or Private Stopham might dream up to surround their nether regions.

Reggie Whymper was still putting on the pressure. 'The NERTS will be in civvies, of course. Dr Roxborough tells me he even has a sporran.'

Captain Pomona enjoyed a brief – *mot juste* – fantasy of SO Preece dressed only in a sporran and fishnet tights.

Dr Whymper brought him back to reality with all the nerve-jarring finality of the chord that alerts those involved that the 'Eightsome' is about to set off on its frenetic, geometrical course.

'I've got a surprise for you, Bertram. I shall be wearing Hunting Ogilvie. I've got an extra skirt and I'm making it into a kind of kilt – for *you.*'

On the night of the dance the full moon entered precisely on cue. It rose from behind the shoulder of Hummel, golden as a Piece of Eight, mysterious behind a veil of sea mist. Graham MacCallister caught his breath when he saw it. Even MacGregor acknowledged that it promised to be a night on which the magic of Ben Dhui would be at its most powerful. When they met outside MacGregor's cottage, Janet Morgan's reaction was predictably practical. 'Visibility for scientific purposes should be excellent,' she said.

'A lassie like you should no be worrying about the private parts of a hind on a night like this. Leave that to yon auld stags. They know what to do, better than some humans I could think of.'

Far away, the opening salvoes of Jimmy Shand smote the night air.

'If you two have a mind to dance,' MacGregor suggested hopefully, 'I could bring my pipes.' He was a great believer in the aphrodisiac qualities of the bagpipes.

'Thank you, MacGregor. Now if you'll just lead the way up to the shearing shed . . .'

'Aye, the shearing shed . . .' His hopes rose briefly.

'I'll go my own way from there,' Janet added.

'Have it your own way, lassie, but you're missing the chance of a lifetime. It's not every rut that the full moon rises bright and clear over Horn.' MacGregor nudged

Graham so hard that he veered off the track. In single file, they set off up the path towards Ben Dhui.

Captain Pomona had decided that his only hope was to enter (a) late and (b) into the spirit of things. The kilt which the MO had adapted for him was short on pleats but, as might be expected of a garment fashioned from an evening skirt formerly designed to surround Regina Whymper, it was long on length. It reached down below the knees, giving him the appearance not so much of a Highland laird as that of a drag artist fitted out by a tent-maker. Pomona waited until both he and the dancers had got several stiff drinks beneath their sporrans before making an entrance.

The MO had gone to town in the most bizarre fashion. The equipment store had been cleared of hundreds of thousands of pounds worth of military accessories, for all of which he was ultimately responsible. The walls were hung with camouflage nets decorated with bunches of heather and, for some totally obscure reason, the long ribbons of the curly seaweed found along the shore after a westerly gale. Suspended from the ceiling was another product of the island's flotsam or possibly jetsam: a row of brightly coloured plastic net floats. Above the bar which stood like a high altar at the far end of the store was a stag's head, recently culled and somewhat inadequately cleaned out by Dr Hulke. The smell was indescribable, the heather and seaweed combining to produce a scent not unlike that of herbal tea. The newly dead stag contributed something of the aroma of a butcher's shop in the backstreets of Katmandu.

Captain Pomona's entrance coincided with a lull in the festivities. Not surprisingly it provoked a loyal, or, anyway, impressed cheer. He felt that it might be appropriate to curtsey by way of acknowledgement but finally bowed rather formally instead. As he did so, his jabot, fashioned by Dr Whymper from the lace from an old pair of French knickers – the bloody woman had been desperately keen to let him know that she wore the ridiculous things – popped out of his service dress jacket like a comic dickey.

'We're just about to start a "Foursome Reel",' Dr Whymper shrieked.

Pomona spotted the flashing thighs of Lieutenant Preece. Thank God, she had decided to wear Scottish fancy dress. The tartan skirt of which Dr Whymper had so vigorously disapproved at dancing class seemed more mini than ever. The exertions of the last evolution, a spirited Duke of Perth, had hitched the rear pleats fetchingly up over her right buttock. Pomona spotted Corporal Dunfee's hand snaking towards the rear thus exposed, fingers poised for a secret pinch. Pomona wondered what the entry on Dunfee's charge sheet might read should he connect with his target and should the owner seriously object. Pinching a commissioned officer's bum? It didn't sound quite official but then nothing about this ghastly evening was remotely official. He avoided the MO's invitation to join the dance and slid quickly between Corporal Dunfee and Lieutenant Preece in order to divert the corporal's dastardly attack.

Dunfee, who couldn't precisely see where his hand was going in the press around the bar, closed his fingers on the rearward aspect of Captain Pomona's Hunting Ogilvie.

Pomona leapt like a heart-shot stag.

'Christ Almighty!' he yelled.

Corporal Dunfee, as was his custom, was several drinks ahead of everyone else.

'I'm verra sorry, sir. I was just admiring a verra nice piece of cloth. You'll take a dram with me, sir?'

'Thank you, corporal.'

'I hope I didn't bruise your arse, sir.'

'That's quite all right, corporal.'

'To tell you the truth, sir, it wasna' intended for you.'

'I rather gathered that.'

'All in the spirit of the evening, sir.'

At this point, 'Butch' Cassidy behind the bar mercifully produced half a tumbler of Scotch. Pomona gulped it down. Even above the opening 'whoops' of the dancers, Pomona's sense-inflamed ears caught the silky susurration of Lieutenant Preece's tights as she moved towards him.

'May I say you're looking very lovely tonight, sir,' she said teasingly.

‘Thank you, Myfanwy. It’s a small thing I had run up for the occasion by a little, or should I say enormous, woman round the corner.’

‘I’d have done it for you. I made my own.’

Pomona looked at the garment in question and felt that faint feeling up the back of his neck again.

‘I shouldn’t have thought you’d have had much material left over.’

‘Enough to make you a pair of tartan underpants. Like mine,’ she added.

Pomona wished to God she’d stop. Even on gala and extension night, officers of the Queen shouldn’t be allowed to carry on like this.

‘What are you wearing underneath by the way?’ Myfanwy asked.

‘Jockey pants. I got them in Edinburgh. They’ve got a thistle printed on the front and the words “Will ye no come back again”.’ He added desperately. ‘They were meant for the tourists.’

‘With a thistle on the front, I shouldn’t think they’d have the strength.’

On the floor, Dr Whymper was marshalling her ‘Foursome’. It consisted of Fergus Roxborough, immaculate in Prince Charles Coatee, setting to Private Stopham; Hammond Hulke, shambolic in his stalker’s thornproof tweed jacket and plus-twos, lecherously encircled a female Scots private with an arm like a giant squid’s tentacle.

Dr Whymper called merrily: ‘You don’t put your arm round your partner until you set to her and swing, Dr Hulke.’

‘I’m swinging already, baby,’ Hulke shouted.

Captain Pomona surveyed the scene of rising revelry with extreme apprehension. Alas, the evening had a long way to go yet.

The hill that night was magical, the moonlight so intense, the heather so brightly lit that the purple in its flowers was almost but not quite visible. The heather reflected a silver sheen, as if touched with a heavy hoar frost. In fact, the air was soft and balmy, thick with scent that would have had a night-flying bee falling out of the sky dead drunk. Graham *was* drunk, drunk with the beauty of Ben Dhui under the full moon, the rutting moon MacGregor had called it. Only one thing was needed to complete his sense of oneness with the natural scene and it, or rather she, was striding unfalteringly along the deer track ten yards ahead of him. Janet's lithe body was outlined in a halo of private moonlight. Was she not affected by the wonder of the night? Did she not feel something of the primeval stirrings that possessed him? Evidently not. When she paused once on the eight hundred foot climb to the shearing shed it was neither for breath nor to draw his attention to the wild grandeur all around them. It was simply to remark; 'Here are some fresh droppings, Graham. Shouldn't you be collecting them?'

Graham ground the small brown pellets flat with his foot as he passed.

When they reached the shearing shed, MacGregor became heavy with what he regarded as tact.

'If you two have anything biological you wish to confer aboot, I wadna' mind seeing if that old ram of mine is hereaboots . . .' He nudged Graham heavily. 'I'll guarantee he no disturbs you by banging against the door. Yon's no respecter of biology, other folk's biology, ye ken.'

Janet said: 'There's nothing to discuss, MacGregor. Mr MacCallister and I both have the scientific disciplines of our research precisely defined.'

'Aye,' said MacGregor sadly. 'I can see you have. You're a disciplined wee lassie, more's the pity. You'll no fall and break your ankle in the darkness. You're sure Mr MacCallister shouldn't . . .'

'Quite sure, thank you. I expect to find a large party of hinds attended by stags about five hundred feet below the south side of the summit.'

'And now, after that little exhibition, we should be ready for the "Eightsome",' Dr Whymper announced with a gaiety close to desperation.

'Though this time we'll take it a little more slowly.' She

shook her finger waggishly, or perhaps wagged her finger shakily, at Hammond Hulke who leant against the bar, one arm clamped around each of his late partners' waists, each hand clasping a pint of McEwan's strong ale. Hulke responded by lifting both his companions clear of the floor and whooping wildly. Then, squeezing the girls tightly to his chest in the manner of King Kong, he somehow managed to drink from both pints at once.

For Hammond Hulke, if for no one else, the 'Foursome' had been a spectacular success. To Fergus Roxborough's fury he had danced practically the whole thing single-handed, setting to everyone including Roxborough, swinging everybody including Roxborough, clearing a tableful of glasses with one of the girl's feet as he whirled her horizontally clear of the ground in a style more reminiscent of an exhibition ice-skater than a Scottish dancer. As a grand finale he had deposited Fergus Roxborough on his kilted backside and slid him under the bar counter. Amazingly, he had managed to do all this more or less in time with the music. On the whole, and with the undoubted exceptions of doctors Roxborough and Whymper, this *tour de force* had been well received. The audience had begun to feel that the evening was hotting up and had distinct possibilities. Even Captain Pomona was enjoying himself, if only because he felt that Regina Whymper was at last getting what she amply deserved. His enjoyment was marred a few seconds later.

'Captain Pomona,' Dr Whymper advanced and seized him by the hand. 'Come along now, Captain Pomona, I need you to lead off the "Eightsome" with me. You're not to worry if you forget the evolutions. I'll call them out to everyone as we go along. Don't forget all you eightsomers how we begin: circle, cartwheel, set to partner, turn, then the chain.'

Captain Pomona's brain performed a reel all of its own. It felt as though it was being chained to a cartwheel, turned *and* circled.

Janet Morgan lay prone in the heather five hundred feet below and to the south of the Tine of Horn. Fifty yards ahead of her, as she had predicted, a herd of over twenty hinds grazed in the moonlight. Just beyond the herd and slightly above them, a ten-pointer patrolled nervously up and down, keeping an eye on his harem. He had coupled with seven hinds since mid-day. He was hungry, tired and apprehensive, yet he knew he could not afford to lower his head to graze for too long, or wander away more than a few yards to find the richest feeding. He was enjoying an extremely unenviable superiority. If he relaxed for more than the blink of an eyelid, he was liable to lose his advantage.

Janet, professionally absorbed by the scene was thankful to Graham for suggesting the night expedition on the hill. She was perfectly placed downwind of the hinds. Nevertheless she would never have found them so easy to approach or so difficult to alarm in broad daylight. She had already filled two pages of notes. Five of the females were in mid-*oestrus*, four more just starting, another three beginning to pass out of season.

She had gleaned all the information possible for the moment. Still watchful, she relaxed for the first time, allowing her body to mould to the firm yet supple embrace of the heather. The wiry stalks brushed nipples moulded by her sweater. She felt an involuntary, almost electrical shock. Graham had been right on several counts: it *was* a magical night. The ten-pointer trotted forward and nosed the rear end of one of the young hinds in her first season. Janet experienced an unexpected but very distinctly sympathetic frisson. Purposefully, she addressed herself to her notebook. This would not do. It simply would not do.

She was, she often assured herself, a perfectly normal, even a romantic female. She was, however, professionally ambitious. She did not for a moment rule out the possibility of love entering her life at a point chosen by herself. That point had not yet been reached and would certainly not be reached on the Island of Horn. In different circumstances, Graham MacCallister might have been quite interesting. He was young, fresh and good-looking, though not, perhaps, as scientifically dedicated as he should be. Yet even he seemed to assume that he was irresistible and that she was bound in the end to fall for him. Well, he, too, would have to be made to see that he was eminently resistible.

That there had been no major terpsichorean contretemps in the 'Eightsome' was largely because Dr Hammond Hulke had been excluded from it. That and the fact that, apart from herself and Bertram Pomona, Dr Whymper had wisely picked her remaining team from the Scottish contingent. True, Captain Pomona had exhibited a certain tendency to get lost and wander off during the cartwheel. As the last chord crashed away, signalling release from the athletic torment of the last ten minutes – or was it ten hours? – there he was, all on his own. Captain Pomona felt that he had better do something Scottish and so he yelled 'Oi', a not especially Scottish syllable, and leapt high into the air. This was too much for his hastily run-up Hunting Ogilvie that promptly slid to the ground leaving him in his green jockey pants.

In his entire military career Bertram Pomona did not recall receiving a standing ovation from his troops.

'That's a bonny wee thistle you've got there, Captain.'

'Och, dinna pluck it, Jeannie. It's got an awfu' powerful prickle to it.'

Amidst this ribaldry, Dr Whymper found herself staring fascinated at this flower of Scotland so unexpectedly revealed. Then she wrapped her tartan sash around Captain Pomona's midriff and bore him off for running repairs.

MacGregor lead the way up the final pitch on the Tine. To Graham's surprise, when they came to the base of the near-vertical wall of rock, MacGregor did not feel for the slender toe- and hand-holds with whose aid Graham was accustomed to reach the summit of Ben Dhui. Instead he led off to the right round the base of the rock pinnacle.

Graham touched him on the shoulder. 'You're not going straight up? I'll lead if you like.'

'I'm no' breakin' my neck at night. Besides, there's a far easier way.'

When they had traversed the base of the Tine, MacGregor pointed upwards. 'After the first few feet it's like climbing a staircase.'

If this was somewhat of an exaggeration, the route, after the first ten feet, was far simpler, almost a beginner's climb. When they reached the top, MacGregor suddenly disappeared, apparently into the heart of the rock itself. When Graham followed he discovered why. The route made an easy entry into the cup at the top of the peak through the natural drain at one end.

'It's nae so guid when it's been raining and snowing, but in fine weather even a lassie can make the climb. Now, if you could have persuaded yon wee female Doctor of Science to climb with you tonight . . .'

'Well, seeing she's somewhere down there and we're up here, the matter doesn't seem to arise.'

'Aye. But if you hear the great stag belling while you're up here alone, or anyway wi' me, you'll have what you want from her.'

Graham strained his ears.

'Not a sound,' he said.

'Mebbe not a sound but sight enough. You'll agree?'

It was true. Beneath a moon so over-full that it seemed to have burst and spilt its silver across the world, the Island of Horn lay set out as if in a strange negative daylight. The moon's silver caught the white crests running in the never-sleeping Race of Horn. The moonlight softened the steep heather-covered steps leading from Ben Dhui to the sea so that they resembled the subtle folds and slopes of a sleeping woman's body. The comparison made him wonder in which of those folds lay the soft, subtle folds that comprised Dr Janet Morgan.

Graham looked across the hump of the islet of Hummel to the south, straining to pick out the outline of the mainland peaks seventy-five miles away.

He put up his night glasses. Yes, there they were. Between the twin mountains two minute snake's eyes glowed red – the warning lights on the chimneys of the new atomic power station at Dundoom.

MacGregor nudged him.

'Hark!'

At first, far off, a stag roared. Then right close at hand came an answering roar. The master stag, the twelve-pointer, was belling defiance right beneath the Tine.

MacGregor was triumphant. 'The wee doctor's yours, lad, and, if I've a mind to it, the bonny Flora's mine.'

In the NCO's mess Corporal Gunnersbury was preparing a punch which, he was confident, would set the seal of social success on the highland dancing. He worked happily emptying almost the entire reserve liquor stocks of the mess into a cookhouse dixie. The resulting punch had a highly distasteful pinkish hue. This was because Corporal Gunnersbury had discovered, just as the punch was coming to the boil, a bottle of peppermint liqueur called Blush Cream which Lance-Corporal Mason had brought back from leave and even CSM Markham had declined to drink. Gunnersbury hoped that the peppermint flavour, if not the pinkish colour, would be disguised by the two bottles of ruby port, the one of elderflower wine, the litre of Spanish *rosé*, and the half gallon of Lance-Corporal Mason's home-brewed brown ale which made up the body of the recipe. He was right. The taste *was* disguised. In its place, the punch had acquired a terrible pink potency. It bubbled like the surface of a soda lake. To top it all off, Corporal Gunnersbury heaved in some sliced lemons and a clove of garlic for luck, praying that these wouldn't dissolve, like portions of a corpse in an acid bath, before he could serve the mixture to the delighted dancers. As a finishing touch, he sprinkled some meths on to the surface, intending to light this on entering the scene of the revels as a final act of showmanship.

The effect was rather more spectacular than even he had hoped for. Acted upon by the seething combination of spirits on which it floated, the meths had vaporised to form a highly explosive gas. At first sight of a naked flame it detonated with a *whoomf* like the firing of a six-inch mortar, removing the corporal's eye-lashes, eyebrows and setting fire to the decorations, including a largish section of camouflage netting, several bunches of heather and a strip of dried seaweed. When all this, including Corporal Gunnersbury had been extinguished, the punch was ladled out into pint mugs and drunk at first with pleasurable anticipation and subsequently in shocked silence.

'Christ!' said CSM Markham, when the first mouthful had hit the bottom of his stomach without, as far as he could tell, actually punching a hole in the lining, 'He's been at the battery acid. I'll get the bastard for this.'

The rest fought for control in their own private and various ways. Most watered at the eyes. Some were taken with a wracking fit of coughing. Butch Cassidy gulped hers down in one, like a man. Captain Pomona wondered how he had come to swallow a live, red-hot crab. Hammond Hulke demanded a second helping. No one sipped. It was too horrible to sip. All, once they had recovered from the initial shock, experienced a febrile rising of the spirits and loosening of the *id*.

Dr Whymper seized the moment to propose what she had long seen as the highpoint and finale of the evening.

'I believe,' she boomed, 'that we are all quite ready for the climax of our little gathering. We have danced the Foursome, we have danced the Eightsome. We shall now conclude with the Sixteensome.'

It was a proposal that might have taken her audience's breath away, had the punch not already done so. Everyone present had now drunk enough to accept that a Sixteensome was not only possible but highly desirable.

Lieutenant Preece now spoke up: 'Why don't we dance it outside? There's a *gorgeous* moon.'

'What a lovely, lovely idea.' Dr Whymper managed to combine total enthusiasm for Lieutenant Preece's suggestion with a glance that expressed total disapproval of Lieutenant Preece. Captain Pomona felt Dr Whymper's jealousy slice down between himself and the delightfully propinquitous Myfanwy like a butcher's cleaver.

'Old cow,' Myfanwy said. 'Don't worry, Bert, I'll stick close to you.'

'Sergeant Major!'

CSM Markham removed his hand from Cecilia Munt's angular rump.

'Please arrange for the loudspeakers to be placed outside. Now, everyone: pick your partners and form up at the rear of store in your sets. Captain Pomona.'

The punch had made Pomona bold. 'Sorry, Regina,' he said. 'I'm afraid my card's filled in for this one.'

The MO was about to protest when a tide of enthusiastic soldiery burst upon her and carried her outside.

Hammond Hulke who had failed to latch on to any spare military crumpet, as he had hoped and forecast, recognised a sex-starved woman when he saw one. He seized hold of Dr Regina Whymper and lead her out. This left Captain Pomona free to move in – though movement was hardly necessary – on Lieutenant Preece. The rest of the Sixteensome fell into couples on predictable lines.

Only Fergus Roxborough appeared to be left out. But not for long. A natural leader among men and an unnatural show-off among women, Roxborough took over, in Dr Whymper's absence, as caller and master of ceremonies.

Myfanwy Preece's suggestion to go outside had been a moment of pure Cymric inspiration. The same moonlight that burned down on Graham, Janet and MacGregor far away high up on Ben Dhui, now turned the unlovely lines of the Equipment Store into a Highland Taj Mahal. Under Fergus Roxborough's direction, the Sixteensome formed up on the parade ground.

'The Sixteensome,' he told them, speaking from an improvised podium on a bale of cotton waste, 'is like the Eightsome only more so. We start with the circle and double cartwheel. Then you set and turn your partners and form two chains, one inside the other . . . All clear so far?'

'All clear,' the dancers yelled, though none save Dr Whymper had the foggiest idea what he was talking about.

'Right. Off we go then.'

Jimmy Shand burst on the night air with all the considerable power at his command.

Somehow, and with blind faith in Dr Roxborough and possibly each other, they joined hands and the great circle began to gyrate.

The time was a quarter to midnight.

At the end of an hour, during which he shared a flask of his special malt with Graham, MacGregor decided that he had been sufficiently exposed to the moonlight of Ben Dhui for its injection of magic to take. When the twelve-pointer had roared close at hand for nigh on twenty minutes without stopping, MacGregor took his leave, via the drainage sump at the north end of the Tine. His parting words were: 'Ye'll find your own way doon, nae doot. Mebbe you'll find the wee Janet too. I'll no wait for ye at the shearing shed. I've a mind to call on a hind of my ain.'

Graham correctly took this to refer to Flora Flodden. Plainly MacGregor had complete faith in the potency of the rutting moon. As a scientist, Graham had to confess that he did not. As a romantic, however, he saw nothing against trying to find Janet on his descent and persuading her to walk back with him. Who knows what effect the braes of Horn under the moon might have had even on her?

It was a quarter to midnight when he finally decided to leave the Tine by MacGregor's exit and nearly twelve when he set out from the base of the rock wall to look for Janet. He expected to find her somewhere around the 2500 foot contour line.

At five minutes to midnight, the Sixteensome whirled to its inebriated close. By the time the last two men had taken their places in the middle, it was, in fact, a Seventeensome. Dr Fergus Roxborough had long since been toppled from his caller's position on top of the bale of cotton waste and had been absorbed, without anyone much noticing, into the rituals and rigours of the dance. The dancers had soon found the miniscule parade ground too small to accommodate their enthusiasm. Centrifugal force had flung them outwards into the peripheral heather. This caused a good deal of tripping and falling down, but no one seemed to mind that very much either.

In fact, the Sixteensome never did reach its final double chain. In the middle of one of the dance's most abandoned whirls, the generator supplying current to both the record player and the lights failed. At that precise moment, happily in their original combinations, couples were whirling away into the heather. They continued to whirl delightedly, *sans* lights, *sans* music, *sans* everything except each other. It was a fitting climax to the evening. Some fell down after only a short distance. Others whirled a good way before a particularly bosky dell offered them the privacy they sought.

The night breeze freshened from the south-east, its sighs merging with the sighs that arose from various parts of the heather.

The time was exactly midnight.

October, First Week

'Christ!' said the Prime Minister, 'not another one.'

The Minister for Energy picked up the decoded cable his leader had just dropped and considered the text with that air of balanced gravity for which he was justly infamous.

'We haven't had one for eighteen months now,' he said with some pride.

'I'd be better pleased if you could arrange for the interval to be at least eighteen years.'

'From what I know of the location, PM,' countered the Minister, 'this one cannot have done very much harm.'

'That's nice then,' said the Prime Minister. 'The voters aren't too taken with the idea of web-footed, two-headed babies.'

The mention of deformities brought the Minister for Health to the alert. She froze like a setter on point, sharp nose and bright eye fixed on the Prime Minister. The illusion of the well-trained hunting dog catching a keen scent was heightened by the fact that her right forearm was raised, hand bent limply at the wrist. It was a favourite mannerism of hers as opponents on the platform and in the House knew to their cost. It managed to convey an air of feminine helplessness which in a second, when arm and limp hand straightened in a gesture of accusation or emphasis, could be transformed to flagrant feminine militancy. The PM saw it, knew it and feared it. He thought he knew how a grouse felt, crouching in a clump of heather in the hope that the setter would not bound forward and flush it to the guns. With the Rt Hon Audrey Margetson he knew he could expect no such escape. Audrey was not only one of the most efficient of his cabinet colleagues, she was one of the most determined and ambitious. She was convinced that she would make a very good job of his own office and hardly bothered to disguise the fact that she intended to fill it some not too distant day.

She smelt blood. With any luck, that of the Minister for Energy's blood group, though she sometimes wondered whether the Minister didn't run exclusively on white corpuscles.

'I think,' she said sweetly, 'I heard the question of a hazard to health mentioned. The PM even talked of abnormalities and deformities.'

She suspected that the pill-pushers had slipped up again. If so, she was, politically speaking, almost certainly in the chips. Wicked international drug cartels, who were careless enough to get their prescriptions wrong, could be made to look as though they were practising genocide against the working classes.

The Prime Minister felt Audrey Margetson's questing nose ruffling the feathers at the back of his neck. He must rely on the guile that had made him such a downy old political bird. If he took off silently and then did a quick jink or two, the Minister for Energy should collect most of the shot and shell that would shortly be flying around.

'There's been another leak,' he said, with just the faintest of emphasis on 'another'.

'Leak of what, might I ask, Minister?' This was from the Chancellor. Leaks always made the Chancellor nervous. It couldn't be his fault this time. In his department, the budget was the prime time for leaks and April was still six months away.

'It appears that there has been some kind of a leak from the new nuclear power station at Dundoom,' the Prime Minister told his colleagues.

'Not necessarily serious,' put in the Minister for Energy.

'How the hell do you know that?' The Chancellor felt he was on safer ground now. There had, thank Mammon, been no mention of missing financial secrets. Dundoom had been one of the Energy Minister's pet projects. The Chancellor had opposed building the place on the perfectly reasonable grounds that the country couldn't afford it. The Ministry for Energy had probably skimped on materials, left out a couple of tons of lead insulation or something.

'How do I know the results are likely to be minimal? Because, Chancellor, we sited the reactor in a situation where any untoward event is likely to be negated by its geographical location.'

'Just where the devil is Dundoom?' The Foreign Secretary felt he could be forgiven for missing out on a few home crisis fronts.

'Dundoom stands well out to sea on a small promontory in the extreme north-western Highlands,' the Minister for Energy explained.

'I think we should consult the maps before we go any further,' suggested the Prime Minister. So his personal private secretary had the maps brought in and spread out on the cabinet table.

The Minister for Energy enthusiastically traced the outline of a slim finger of land pointing in the general direction of Labrador.

'You can see how any leakage of radiation or anything else must proceed harmlessly out to sea.'

'What about the fish?' Audrey Margetson wanted to know. 'People eat fish,' she added a little unnecessarily, but felt the point had to be made.

'They're not affected.'

'I'd like to challenge that statement.'

'I'm sure you would, Audrey,' the Prime Minister had decided that he could let the pressure down a bit by scattering a few Christian names around. 'And no doubt you *should* challenge it, but we don't want to get away from the point. Has this leakage at Dundoom done any local damage?'

'The latest report I have received,' said the Minister for Energy, 'assures me that the leak was detected at 2200 hrs. last night, the fault remedied and all made secure by 0330.'

'Correct me if I'm wrong, Ted,' the Prime Minister had to make a great effort to call Edward Illingworth, Minister for Energy, by the name by which he was known to his friends, or, as some said, friend.

'Correct me if I've got it wrong, but this lethal whatever it was was loose for five and a half hours.'

'We don't know that it *was* lethal.'

'Do we know anything about the radiation in question?'

'It wasn't radiation, well not in that exact form anyway.'

The Prime Minister experienced a momentary spasm of relief. From what he knew of radiation it got around everywhere like radio waves. There was no stopping the stuff.

'Preliminary results suggest it was a kind of gas.'

The Prime Minister knew all about gas. Nasty stuff which needed a bit of atmospheric help to spread it about. A sinister thought struck him.

'If it was a radioactive gas, wouldn't it be carried on any wind that was blowing?'

'Precisely, Prime Minister.'

'Precisely what, or rather where?'

'Out to sea, Prime Minister.'

'How do you know that?'

'My planners had that in mind when we chose the site. The prevailing wind is from the south-south-east. Nine days out of ten it blows from that quarter.'

'And on the night in question?'

'During the last two hours I have had full reports from the Meteorological Department. The wind freshened in early evening and by 2000 hrs. it was blowing strongly from the prevailing direction.'

'Out to sea?'

'Exactly, Prime Minister.'

Audrey Margetson asked: 'What about ships in the area?'

'We've already checked. There were none, not even fishing boats.'

'And North America?'

'The gas would have lost its effect after two hundred miles.'

The Prime Minister decided to pontificate a little at Ted's expense.

'On this occasion we seem to have been very lucky. However, this Government, indeed any Government cannot, in matters of this gravity, afford to rely on luck.'

The Prime Minister paused. It was intended to be a pregnant pause whose warm comfortable womb was filled with a warm uncomfortable warning. It was the Minister for Scottish Affairs who performed the abortion.

'Well,' he said, 'perhaps we should just look at the map a mite more closely. Scotland, you know, is famous for both its Highlands and islands.'

A weight like an under-cooked haggis stirred in the pit of the Minister for Energy's stomach.

'We're miles clear of the Hebrides, both Inner and Outer. Rockall is too far out and anyway there's no one on it.'

'Mebbe,' the Minister's Glaswegian accent only became pronounced in political speeches made north of the Border or when scoring points off Sassenach friends and foes. 'Mebbe we should just take a look at the map to be cairtain. South-south-east.' He laid a ruler on the required bearing, starting at Dundoom.

With fascinated eyes the company followed the straight edge as it led out to sea. Where the ruler stopped and slap in the middle of its blunt end were two dots, one considerably larger than the other.

'Where the hell is that?' the Prime Minister demanded.

The Scotsman affected to read the names with difficulty, taking off his half glasses, and squinting at the small print.

'Horn,' he announced. 'The Island of Horn. And the lesser islet, if I'm not mistaken, is a lump of rock called Hummel.'

'Never heard of them,' thundered the Prime Minister as if this declaration would automatically remove them from the map. 'I suppose they're uninhabited. A few goats and that sort of thing.'

'Well now . . .' began the Minister for Scottish Affairs.

'They're too far off the mainland and far too small for anyone to live there.' The Minister for Energy sounded confident but then, as past events had often proved, this was no guarantee of a happy outcome.

'Distant and small. Hummel is certainly all of that,' the Scot agreed. 'But if you will cast your mind back, Prime Minister . . .'

The Prime Minister was frantically doing so. The word Horn had blown a toot of warning in his ear.

'Wasn't there some trouble with the Scots about Horn?' he demanded.

'That was in my predecessor's time, I recollect, Prime Minister, when the Ministry of Defence proposed to put a Radar Tracking Unit on the island.'

'And did they?'

'I rather think they did, Prime Minister.'

'Is it still there?'

'Perhaps we ought to call them in and ask them.'

'NERTS!' said the Minister for Health abruptly.

The Prime Minister was used to this sort of rudery in the House but he was damned if he was going to take it in the Cabinet room.

'I *beg* your pardon, Minister,' he said coldly.

Audrey Margetson smiled sweetly. 'NERTS!' she said again.

'Do you mind explaining what seems a rather irrelevant and, I must say, uncharacteristically childish comment?'

'Certainly Prime Minister. NERTS or rather NERT. The National Environmental Research Trust, collectively, I believe known as THE NERTS. They're on the island, too. You may remember Sir Irwin Broadchalke lobbying us to allow his scientists on to Horn to study deer, I believe. It was just after the Army moved in.'

The Minister for Energy's white corpuscles had rushed to his face. His look of bland confidence had bleached several shades.

The Prime Minister spoke gravely and slowly. It was the voice he used to suggest to his colleagues that they had once again betrayed his trust with their incompetence.

'Am I to understand then that there are a number of people who may have been exposed to this . . . to whatever it was?'

The Minister for Energy rallied weakly: 'We're by no means certain that whatever it was actually reached Horn.'

'Then we'd better find out.' With a great effort, the Prime Minister managed to sound incisive. 'We'll reconvene at 1500 hrs. Ted, I want the latest report from Dundoom. Get hold of whoever's responsible for Horn at the MOD. Oh yes, and find the best meteorological man the Air Ministry can provide. I don't have to tell you that all this is under wraps.' He couldn't resist a dig at the Minister of Energy. 'We don't want any more leaks, do we, Ted?'

The three o'clock meeting was commendably brief.

The Met. man established beyond doubt that a wind Force four to five would have carried any gas released at Dundoom on a narrow front that must have covered both Hummel and Horn.

Next, the Brigadier-General in charge of Scottish Tracking Stations reported that Army personnel on Horn numbered eleven women and ten men. Four NERTS and two civilians brought the total to twenty-seven persons.

'Has the commanding officer on Horn reported anything untoward, Brigadier?'

'No, sir. The station is operational and appears to be functioning normally.'

'Well, I suppose it would,' Ted Illingworth said doubtfully.

'What do you mean by that?'

'Well any after-effects – I mean if there *is* anything to affect anyone afterwards – would take a bit of time to show up.'

The Prime Minister felt himself panicking.

'I don't want you chaps panicking. We've all got to stay calm. The public is very rightly nervous about this sort of thing. And talking of knowing more, Illingworth, perhaps your scientist colleagues have found out what it was your people let loose up there last night.'

'They haven't precisely analysed the leakage yet, Prime Minister. An extremely rare plutonium isotope appears to have found its way into a perfectly normal stream of waste gas.'

'What effect would this extremely rare plutonium isotope have on perfectly normal people? Would it,' asked the Prime Minister with desperate sarcasm, 'tend to cause a genetic mutation producing a new generation of web-footed, two-headed babies?'

'Hardly that Prime Minister.'

'Then what?'

'Until we isolate the source and nature of the radiation

we can't be sure. As far as we can say at the moment it appears to belong to a category that might affect hormonal balance.'

'You mean that men might start growing . . .' the Prime Minister found his gaze inexplicably zeroed in on Audrey Margetson's justly renowned upperworks. He caught himself quickly . . . 'start developing female characteristics.'

'It's possible, Prime Minister.'

'And vice versa, I take it.'

'Also possible, Prime Minister. But as I say we can't be sure. For one thing it would depend on the intensity of the radiation and the degree of exposure.'

The Prime Minister was feeling a little better. Two-headed babies were something the public wouldn't stand for. The way things were going in the country, he couldn't see that a few more transvestites and drag artistes would make much difference.

'Ted, you'd better arrange to visit the power station immediately. For the moment, nothing is to be released to the press. Routine checks and maintenance are simply being carried out. Oh, I nearly forgot. Was anyone exposed to the possible effects of the leakage at Dundoom?'

'I have the report you asked for here, Prime Minister. It appears that only one person could have been at risk. A security guard called Gilbey was on duty in a watch hut at the extreme end of the promontory. My department thinks it advisable, in view of the nuclear nature of the power station, to keep a watch to seaward for possible intruders.'

'Yes, yes,' the Prime Minister said testily. 'I expect the Russians are planning a combined operation to steal the reactor at this very moment. Thank God for Gilbey.'

'Gilbey's hut was, of course, directly downwind of the chimneys that released the gas.'

'So he got the full dose?'

'Very improbably, Prime Minister. The waste gas is a very light one and the chimneys are two hundred and fifty feet high. The hut is four hundred yards from their base. It is very unlikely the gas would drop much in a Force Four wind within that distance.'

'I don't need to be told about the square on the

hypotenuse, Ted. What I want to know about is Gilbey.'

'Perfectly normal so far – except for one thing.'

The Prime Minister was horrified. He already had visions of a security guard with a third eye developing in the middle of his forehead, useful perhaps in his type of work but hardly conducive to public peace of mind if it got out.

'For God's sake. What's abnormal about the chap?'

'Well, apparently he's usually a very placid individual. But this morning when he reported for work, he rushed at his shop steward and butted him in the pit of the stomach.'

'That sounds like an Alpha plus for normality to me,' the Prime Minister said sadly.

'Wearing his Securicor crash helmet, Prime Minister?'

The Prime Minister made one of his on-the-spot decisions.

'Isolate Gilbey,' he ordered, 'and keep him under close observation.'

The morning after the Highland dancing, Captain Pomona presided over his orderly room as usual. He tried hard to concentrate on what CSM Markham was saying. He felt a little out of sorts. That awful punch Corporal Gunnersbury had concocted had a great deal to answer for. He had a wide experience of hangovers but this was the first time he had encountered one that produced a terrible dual irritation on the crown of the head. The punch had been responsible for far worse than that. He winced at the memory of what had overtaken him out there in the scented heather. Just when he was certain that he and Lieutenant Preece were set to make a second chorus of *Amazing Grace* together, she had sat up, buttoned her blouse, tossed her head at him and, for no apparent reason, stalked away into the darkness. Captain Pomona had been conscious of no short-coming on his part. All he had experienced was a temporary feeling of faintness and a pronounced singing in the ears. When he had recovered from his frustration he had rushed after her only to stumble into other scurrying figures in the moonlight. Though he retained a confused impression of the scene, he recalled that he was surprised to find so many of the recent dancers in a vertical, peripatetic attitude. He would have expected them to have remained horizontally entwined, as he himself would have wished to be, for some time yet.

CSM Markham coughed to catch his OC's attention.

'About Corporal Gunnersbury, sir.'

'Yes, CSM.'

'We were discussing what we should do about the punch.'

'Throw it away, CSM. It made me feel very odd.'

'With respect, sir, we drank it all.'

'Oh, then that accounts for it.'

'I've no doubt of that, sir. One or two of the men – and women – have been behaving very oddly, sir. I mean last night, sir, Private Munt positively refused to . . .'

'I don't wish you to tell me anything you might regret, CSM.'

'Thank you, Sir. Can't think what came over me – or her.'

'Tell me, CSM. Are your ears giving you trouble?'

'They're singing a bit, sir. I really think we ought to put Gunnersbury on a charge, sir. Meths is highly dangerous stuff.'

'Yes. I see. Well, I'll consider it. Anything wrong, Sergeant-Major?'

The CSM, who had been standing rigidly to attention, had snatched off his cap and thrown it to the ground. He was furiously scratching the crown of his head.

Graham MacCallister was the only male NERT who was unable to blame Corporal Gunnersbury's punch for the way he felt the morning after the dance. The events of the previous night were now like a partly remembered dream. He recalled everything with the utmost clarity until he had begun the long descent through the heather from the top of Ben Dhui. Thereafter things had become as hazy as the moonlight in which they had taken place. Only the headache and the singing in the ears remained this morning to convince him that something unusual had happened to his normally iron constitution up there on Ben Dhui.

*

Hammond Hulke interrupted his musings by throwing open the door with his shoulder.

'Steady, Hammond.'

'Want to make something of it, youngster?'

Hammond had an unnaturally wild look about him.

'I've just had to sort Fergus out,' he said. 'Told him that next time I'd put some weight behind it.'

'Behind what?'

'My shoulder! I just gave him a gentle shove to warn him. Sent him flying out of the back door of the cottage.'

'Good God, Hammond. What for?'

'Nosing around too close to the lovely Janet, youngster.'

'He's always doing that, and, by the by, Hammond, do you mind not calling me youngster?'

'Well, you are, aren't you? You're just a pricket, aren't you?' A pricket, as Hammond Hulke realised Graham would know, was a young stag. Nevertheless he felt he had to elaborate. 'You're certainly more of a pricket than a fully grown prick, if you know what I mean, and I'm sure you do.'

'I say, Hammond, I find that rather offensive even by your somewhat uncouth standards.'

'You know what to do if you don't like it.'

'Have you been drinking, Hammond?'

'Not since last night. I say, that stuff the Army served up packed a hell of a punch . . . hell of a punch, eh, rather good that.' He threw his head back and guffawed. Hulke's laugh was more like a stag's roar than usual.

'What happened last night, Hammond?'

'What happened? An awful lot happened. Dr Vagina Whymper happened for a start.'

Graham was fascinated despite the fact that whatever revelation Hulke was about to make was certain to be in the worst possible taste.

'You mean, she . . .?'

'Hard up as I am for a slice of crumpet on this Scottish Alcatraz, I can't say that I've ever cast an exactly lascivious eye on La Whymper. I thought the old bag had the hots for Bertie Pomona. But last night out there in the heather after the dance . . .'

'Really.'

'She's never given me a second glance before, but last night . . . well, it was as if she'd suddenly come into season. Quite a performance.' He added graphically. 'What a bang!'

'More of a bang than a Whymper.'

'Very well put that.'

'Thanks. Actually, that's the way T. S. Elliot said the world ends.'

'If she goes on like that, I shouldn't be at all surprised if he's right.'

Forty-eight hours later, Captain Pomona's ear had stopped singing. Not only that but his skull had ceased to itch. CSM Markham, too, was relieved to find that he could hear quite distinctly and that the irritation that had caused him to throw his cap on the orderly room floor had subsided. At one point he had imagined that he felt two little lumps about four inches apart on the front of his skull. Since these appeared to be the epicentre of the irritation, he dismissed them as cleg bites acquired out there in the heather during his unsuccessful Highland Games with Cecilia Munt.

Despite the fact that his itching and ear-singing had disappeared, Pomona felt mysteriously off-colour. So much so that he had decided to take the ultimate risk and consult the MO.

Pomona knocked timidly on Dr Whymper's door. A shriek of girlish laughter obliterated the sound of his feeble rapping. The trilling laugh was unmistakably Myfanwy's. Equally identifiable was the sonorous booming of the MO's chortle. What the hell could the rivals for his attention have found that gave common cause for merriment?

Captain Pomona knocked more boldly and entered. The sight that met his eyes caused him to rub them in astonishment. He had always feared that Gunnersbury's punch would work its way to the sight if not to the brain. Now it appeared to be affecting both.

The MO was sitting on one side of the table, Lieutenant Preece on the other. Between them lay that ultimate symbol of female chummyness, a well-laid, well-spread tea tray, complete with lace cloth, the MO's own private bone china, the remains of a plate of thinly cut cucumber sandwiches and a tin of Bourbon biscuits. As Pomona entered, the MO was in the act of offering Myfanwy a silver box containing Gauloises, her own favourite brand of cigarette.

From the benign, relaxed expression on Myfanwy's seductive features, she was plainly enjoying the MO's company enormously.

'Do I interrupt a consultation?' Pomona asked.

'On the contrary. Myfanwy and I were just enjoying a lovely girl-to-girl talk.'

'Regina and I find we've so much in common.' Myfanwy allowed the MO to light her Gauloise with a gold Ronson. 'A present from an admirer?' she asked.

'Oh come now,' Dr Whymper protested delicately. It was the sort of delicacy with which an ice-breaker approaches a tabular berg. 'You're the one who has all the admirers.'

'I haven't noticed you being exactly overlooked, Regina.' Myfanwy Preece was positively simpering. Could this be the girl who only two nights before had snarled 'jealous old cow,' as her present tea companion attempted to prise Captain Pomona from her side?

'I'll come back another time,' Pomona said. 'When you're less involved.'

At any other time Regina would have cut off his retreat with elephantine flutterings.

'You do that, Bert.'

Before he could leave, the door flew open and there stood Dr Hammond Hulke.

For no reason that he could explain, Pomona turned and rushed at Hulke, striking him a glancing blow on the shoulder. Hulke remained unmoved by so much as a centimetre at the impact. Pomona, however, cannoned off the door post and, tripping on the foot which Hulke neatly extended, tottered off, clawing for balance down the corridor. When he reached his quarters, he poured himself a large tot of malt. His scalp had begun to itch and his ears were singing again. What had possessed him to rush headlong at Hulke? The impulse had been quite uncontrollable. The sooner he saw a doctor, and preferably not Dr Whymper, the better. He rubbed his shoulder. It felt distinctly tender. He was going to have a nasty bruise there.

Jerry Mathews knocked on Joanna Bromley's door in the NERTS cottage she shared with Janet Morgan.

'Feel like a little lek?' Even for him, Jerry Mathews felt quite unusually lekkish.

Joanna scarcely looked up from a two-month-old copy of *Woman & Home*. He had never known her read anything before except Bryan Nelson on gannets, occasionally lightened with a sprinkling of literary guano from Harold Robbins.

'Sorry,' she said. 'I'm going lekking with Flora. By the way, there's a lovely recipe here for apple crumble. Flora's going to teach me to make haggis.'

'Never mind the haggis, or the black pudden for that matter. How about a little lek?' He flapped his arms to stir her memory. At other times his mime would have provoked this lovely bosomy bird of his into making an openly erotic response.

'I told you. Flora and I are going together.'

Jerry tried again: 'I'm a lovely old blackcock, remember?'

'Apart from that being demonstrably untrue,' she said, 'I regard racist jokes of that sort as being in very poor taste.'

'Christ, Joanna! Have you gone bananas?'

'Certainly not. It's just that quite suddenly I have come to see lekking in its true light. So when MacGregor announced that there would be a lek this afternoon . . .'

'What the hell has MacGregor got to do with it? Oh, I see.' Jerry brightened. 'He and Flora. You and me. So long as it's not a hen-swapping party.'

Joanna stared at him coldly. 'There's no question of it being just the four of us. It's the whole Scottish contingent. They all wish to build up a lek.'

'Build one up?'

'Well, it takes time. You should know that. Quite a lot of display by the cocks, perhaps for several days, before anything actually happens. But then, it's your study not mine.'

'When I lek,' Jerry told her desperately trying to get the conversation back on to a properly frivolous level, 'it doesn't take much time to build up anything.' Plaintively, 'Joanna, I do feel like a lovely lek.'

'To call a lek "lovely" is entirely anthropomorphic,' she told him primly. 'Leks are part of the process of natural selection. I should have thought you, of all people, wouldn't have to be told that.'

'I don't, believe me.'

'Well then, stop being irresponsible. I suppose if you want to come with Flora and me I can't stop you.'

'I wouldn't miss an opportunity to lek for anything,' he told her, fearing that this was exactly what he was about to do.

CSM Markham stared darkly out of the orderly room window at the morning muster of his unit. Corporal Gunnersbury called the parade to attention. A new intake of Brownies could have produced a more concerted attempt at bringing the left foot up to the right. Normally, the CSM's reaction would simply have been one of professional disgust tempered by resignation. These were, after all, not real soldiers. They were the sort of chaps and birds who should be twiddling knobs in some commercial television studio, perhaps even working for the BBC. This day, however, he felt an almost ungovernable fury. They needed smartening up. Maybe the girls couldn't help it. He watched Private Stopham's attempts to keep her legs together at the position of attention, reflecting bitterly that where he was concerned she had performed the movement a good deal more sharply and effectively. No, it was the men who needed knocking into shape and he, CSM Markham was the man to do the job. He rushed out on to the miniature square just as Corporal Gunnersbury was about to dismiss the parade.

'As you were, Corporal. I'll take over. 'Tenshun. As you were. 'Tenshun. Now listen to me, you half-hard rabble of knob-twisters. You're a bloody shambles. You so-called radar experts look as though you've fallen asleep watching Coronation Street. I doubt if you'd spot a Russian rocket if it came through the bloody roof. Ladies . . .' he made the most of the distinction . . . 'you look like a Women's Institute on a visit to an Old People's Home. What you need, all of you, is shaking up. Exercise. You don't get enough of it. The right sort I mean . . . Stop smirking, Private Stopham. Okay. Stand at ease while I tell you what I'm going to do for a start. At 1400 hrs. today you will all parade in PT gear.'

'But we've done Scottish dancing for this week,' Private Prendergast said sweetly.

'Quiet! This isn't Scottish dancing. It's unarmed combat. It's time you lot learned to look after yourselves.'

'I'm not going to wrestle with any men,' Private Stopham announced unexpectedly.

'Not even with me?' Corporal Gunnersbury sounded plaintive.

'Particularly not with you.'

'What's come over you suddenly, Gwladys?'

'If you have quite finished discussing your sordid personal relationships . . .'

The parade fell momentarily silent if only because to a man, to a woman, they had found that previously reliable personal relationships appeared to have undergone an unaccountable change in the last forty-eight hours.

'Sergeant-Major, may I ask a question?'

'Yes, Private Munt.'

'Why do we have to learn unarmed combat?'

Two days ago, CSM Markham would have caught a hint of pleasures to come in Cecilia Munt's question. After all, they'd already enjoyed two of the best of three falls together. The third, out there in the heather in the moonlight, had been strictly a non-contest. He saw now that the expression on the stratospheric Private Munt's face spoke of nothing but blank, outraged military curiosity.

'Why do you have to learn unarmed combat?' he repeated. 'Because the Russians might try to land here and steal our highly secret apparatus at any moment.'

In the past the mere mention of an apparatus, let alone a

secret one, would have raised a giggle from someone. The parade remained stony-faced.

'Parade, Dis-*miss*!'

As the tracking unit trooped untidily away to its tea break, CSM Markham admitted to himself that when he had rushed out of his office the idea of teaching unarmed combat had been the remedy bottom-most in his mind. He was not even sure if he knew any unarmed combat. For some reason, coming face to face with Corporal Gunnersbury and Lance-Corporal Mason among the gaggle of assorted females had made him suddenly want to bash the living daylights out of both of them.

Jerry Mathews followed twenty yards behind Joanna and Flora along the steep, winding path towards the shearing shed. For the first quarter of a mile he tried to walk beside the two women. The path was too narrow for comfortable three-abreast progress. But this was not the main reason that he had fallen behind. It soon became very clear that he wasn't wanted.

As Jerry topped the final rise, a strange scene lay revealed in a grassy hollow one hundred feet below him. He had often thought that this place with its soft hidden meadow would have made an ideal lekking ground. Yet the blackcock had never used it. That situation was now being put to rights and in a very unusual fashion. MacGregor sat on top of an immense granite boulder playing his bagpipes, skirling and reeling fit to bust. The antics of the dancers for whom he was playing bore no resemblance to any reel or Strathspey taught in Dr Whymper's classes. And yet, in its general abandonment and wild repetitive rituals there were echoes of the gestures and posturings of Highland dancing. For Jerry Mathews the dance suggested a more basic familiarity. The performers were all men. Waiting on the sidelines and occasionally making tentative and provocative forays on to the dancing ground were Jeannie McCall and her fellow Amazons. It was the men, however, who were making and setting the pace. While he watched, Fergus Roxborough rushed at Corporal Dunfee, raising and fluttering his kilt so that his white jockey pants were bared to the sky. In reply, Corporal Dunfee flashed his backside, then dropping his kilt, whirled about, shoulders raised, hands and forearms drooping. In different parts of the meadow, the other men rushed about using little scuttling steps that made them all look as if they were on roller-skates. Jerry Mathews had watched the scene many times before in the course of his studies. There was no doubt that he was witnessing a blackcock lek, adapted to the limited plumage and display abilities of a group of Highland dancers.

Joanna and Flora had reached the edge of the lekking ground. He would have expected that Joanna, with her previous experience of lek-mime, would have plunged straight in. Quite the contrary. She minced coyly about on the edge of the dancers. She was behaving exactly like a female black grouse, a greyhen, when first arriving at a lek. Jerry experienced a moment's relief that she hadn't immediately responded to the most splendid cock bird performing the mating dance. With his Stuart tartan, swinging sporran, ornamental dirk, iron-grey hair and fine, braw calves there could be little doubt who held this title – Fergus Roxborough.

Flora Flodden showed no such reticence. Using her highly effective travelling step, she shimmied out among the cavorting males. At the sight of Flora flaunting herself MacGregor leapt fifteen feet from his rock, pipes playing, ribbons fluttering, kilt bellying like a parachute. Thus, many a time, had Jerry witnessed male black grouse soaring in from the treetops in the dawn light to begin their dance. Without losing a note, MacGregor rushed at Roxborough, sending him sprawling in the heather.

For the first few minutes Jerry watched the scene with the detached interest of an ornithologist. Suddenly he experienced a mad, overwhelming urge to join them. It was almost as if he had acquired, against his will, the instincts and programmed behavioural urges of a blackcock. He made the movements as if to flare his kilt and flaunt his underpants in imitation of the blackcock's magnificently spread tail coverts and snowy-white tail. As he did so he realised that he was wearing jeans.

MacGregor stopped playing and gave Jerry the sort of look a MacDonald reserves for a Campbell. Then MacGregor dropped his pipes and fell upon him. A few seconds later so did all the other males on the lek. His tee-shirt was ripped off. Someone pulled one leg of his jeans off below the knee. Someone else debagged him of what remained of his trousers. His underpants disappeared with a tearing sound. A boot connected with his skull.

When he came to he was lying naked in the grass. His fellow lekkers had all disappeared. He began to gather up what was left of his clothing. Something of his scientific detachment returned. Plainly, to the other lekkers, he had been in non-breeding plumage, if not actually of an alien species.

CSM Markham's unarmed combat parade that afternoon did not so much fall in as gather. The women did most of the gathering, huddled in two little herds as if they especially needed or, anyway, sought each other's company. Corporal Gunnersbury on the other hand stayed remote between the two groups, pacing warily as if expecting Lance-Corporal Mason, who edged around the outskirts of the smaller party of women, to rush at him. What they were both waiting for, in fact, though perhaps neither of them realised it, was the entrance of CSM Markham.

On the dot of 1400 hrs. the CSM rushed out of the orderly room holding a chair in front of him and lashing it about in the general direction of Corporal Gunnersbury. Three paces short of his target he stopped and began to bellow in a hoarse and totally incomprehensible manner. It was not unlike the sound made by bayonet-fighting instructors when encouraging their pupils to eviscerate hostile sacks. It was also remarkably similar to the roar of a rutting stag.

Corporal Gunnersbury was the first to make his play, stepping sideways between the CSM and Mavis Prendergast.

CSM Markham's reaction was swift and horrible. Rolling his eyes and roaring loudly, he charged, holding the chair with its legs bracketing the area occupied by the corporal's private parts. At the last minute, Gunnersbury side-stepped again, causing the CSM to ram the chair legs through the wall of the orderly room.

'Would you, you bastard?' It was a superfluous question, seeing that the corporal not only would, but had. Seizing the respite offered by the CSM's need to extricate the remaining two legs of the chair from the hut wall, Gunnersbury nipped into the mess hall and grabbed a chair of his own. He now faced his rival with four points to the CSM's two.

Privates Prendergast and Stopham gasped with admiration and shifted their ground towards the corporal.

It was Lance-Corporal Mason's turn. 'Okay, you sods. If that's the way you want it, I'm getting a chair, too. No bugger's going to chiv me with his antlers.'

Gunnersbury and Markham met antler to antler with a shattering clash. Like bayonet fighters, or more possibly stags, they withdrew their points and charged again. Interlocked, they swayed from side to side, grunting horrifically, panting, eyes rolling, each trying to twist his rival off balance.

Lance-Corporal Mason saw his moment and charged from the flank, smashing Corporal Gunnersbury's chair to firewood and goring the CSM severely in the flank.

For the moment, Lance-Corporal Mason commanded the field. While the CSM rolled on the ground clasping his ribs and bellowing, Corporal Gunnersbury, with a single fore-shortened leg left to his chair, fled.

Lance-Corporal Mason advanced on the assembled females. He seemed inclined to drive them towards the scene of earlier victories, the equipment store. For several seconds he stood roaring in triumph. It was a fatal mistake. Captain Pomona, attracted by the commotion, arrived at the orderly room window in time to witness his downfall. A huge, shaggy shape, moving so fast that it was just a coloured blur, thundered into view between the huts and, catching Lance-Corporal Mason from behind, hurled him chair and all through the orderly room door to pitch at Captain Pomona's feet.

Hammond Hulke halted, pawed the ground and then, encircling Privates Stopham and Bond with a hairy arm apiece, whirled them off to the equipment store and slammed the door.

Captain Pomona regarded the scarcely breathing Lance-Corporal with distaste. Then his responsibility to his men reasserted itself. He turned the body over with his foot to make sure it was still breathing. His military training just, but only just, overcame a raving urge to dash outside and commandeer the women not already captured by Hulke.

Had Corporal Gunnersbury, finding the scene of carnage totally deserted by dangerous rivals, not come sneaking back, chairless, at that moment, he might well have done so. Pomona hurried to his quarters, locked the door, poured himself a treble malt and knocked it back in one. He had often imagined that he commanded a troop of sex maniacs. Now, it appeared, for sex you could substitute, or rather add, the word 'homicidal'. The terrible thing was that he appeared, due to forces entirely beyond his control or comprehension, to be in danger of joining them.

Graham MacCallister put his head round Janet's work-room door.

'Can I come in for a moment?'

'Help yourself.'

If the welcome wasn't that of a girl burning with passion, it was at least ten degrees warmer than he was used to. The last few days, he fancied, she had been slightly less stand-offish.

'Janet. Have you noticed anything strange lately?'

Those grave, green eyes regarded him with rather more scientific objectivity than he cared for.

'Strange?'

'I mean have you noticed anything odd about anyone, yourself for instance?'

'I've had a bit of a headache, that's all.'

'That's amazing.'

'Is it?'

'I've had one, too.'

Janet said sharply, 'Two people with a simultaneous headache doesn't strike me as being beyond the bounds of reasonable chance.'

Graham tried another approach. 'Have your ears been singing?'

'A bit. On and off. Why?'

'Mine have, too.'

'Amazing,' said Janet sarcastically.

'Seen anything of Fergus and the dreaded Hulke lately?'

'Not much.'

'Doesn't that strike you as strange?'

'Not really. They're probably out on the hill.'

'Too true, they are,' Graham said this with a vehemence which seemed to come from outside himself, 'Hulke's probably roaring away at this very moment.'

'Well, that's nothing unusual. At least it's a pleasure not to have him roaring away, as you call it, around me.'

'Fergus is never here either. What's changed them? That's what I want to know.'

This time Janet made a remark that seemed to come from outside herself and which was utterly out of character.

'They probably sense I'm not in a state of *oestrus*.' Janet blushed deeply. 'I mean that I'm not attracted to them.'

'Dr Morgan, that was not a very scientific observation. Females of the species *Homo sapiens* do not achieve a state of *oestrus*, more's the pity.'

'You'd all be sorry if they did. Hinds are only on heat for three or four days.'

'I agree. I'd much rather have one lovely, loving all-the-year-round human female.'

Graham didn't have a chance to develop this promising line. The door flew open. Jerry Mathews leant against the door post for support. He was naked to the waist and smeared with peaty soil. His jeans were minus their right leg. One buttock was exposed to the early evening air.

'Good God, Jerry. What happened?'

'I've been lekked,' Jerry said. He wiped a smear of dried blood off his chest.

'By what? By whom?'

'By a lot of randy blackcock, that's who. Just because I was in non-breeding plumage.'

Janet took his arm kindly. 'Come on, Jerry. You're distraught. You've had a fall or something. Perhaps you're concussed. I'll get Joanna.'

Jerry shied away. 'Christ no. Not Joanna. She's off lekking with the others.'

Graham said: 'I'd better get the poor old lad to bed. He's probably been at MacGregor's pot-stilled malt.'

As Graham led Jerry Mathews next door, Fergus Roxborough came swinging up the rock path that served the little line of cottages for a village street. He looked tired and dishevelled, but there was an air of ineffable cockiness about him. His kilt swung. His sporran twitched.

'Christ!' Graham said out loud. 'If anyone looks like a randy old blackcock, it's Fergus.'

Jerry was too far gone to comment. If he could have spoken, he would certainly have agreed.

CSM Markham saluted with his left hand to ease the strain on two right ribs held together with sticking plaster.

'Would it be better if you sat down, Sergeant-Major?'

'Sorry, sir. No chairs. All smashed up.' The mere act of speaking made the CSM grimace with pain.

'Er, quite. Wasn't your unarmed combat session yesterday a little, well perhaps I should say a great deal, too violent? How is Corporal Gunnersbury by the way?'

'Broken arm, sir.'

'My point exactly, Sergeant-Major. This isn't a commando unit you know. We're supposed to be technical experts. At this rate I won't have any NCOs left. I'm afraid these contests will have to stop.'

'Not possible, sir.'

Pomona experienced a barely controllable compulsion to jump across the desk and butt his injured CSM in the stomach.

'Not possible,' he snarled. 'Of course it's possible. I shall just give a direct order. There will be no more of these ridiculous unarmed combat classes.'

'With respect, sir. That's beyond your control. You can't just order nature about.'

'Can't I, by God! What's natural about bashing the living daylights out of each other?'

'Entirely natural, sir. I daresay you're thinking you'd like to have a go at me.'

Markham detected from the sudden look of astonished panic in his OC's eye that this was exactly what he had been thinking.

Pomona pulled himself together. 'Officers do not engage in fisticuffs with senior NCOs.'

'Quite natural, sir. No bad feeling if you did. Not a military matter, sir. Besides the girls love it. Turns them on, at least turns some of 'em on, those that are due to be turned on.'

Pomona wiped his hand across his sweating brow. He looked around for a weapon, fearing he might have to defend himself and in some strange way half-hoping it would come to that.

'What about Lance-Corporal Mason?'

'He's seeing to the MO now.'

'Don't you mean, the MO's seeing to him?'

'Doesn't necessarily follow, sir. Definite signs that she's coming on herself, sir.'

'Christ, I hope not,' Pomona said, though he was by no means sure what he meant by this. He appeared to be the only one to whom the general picture wasn't entirely clear. He tried again.

'What's the extent of Mason's injuries?'

'Suspected dislocated elbow, sir. Won't stop him, though.'

'Stop him *what*?'

CSM Markham remained as rigidly at attention as his cracked ribs would allow and said nothing. Pomona decided to let it pass.

'The whole thing seems to have got ridiculously out of hand. I'm by no means certain that I shouldn't put you all on a charge. I'll certainly have to make a report. These injuries will have to figure in my daily SITREP . . . I suppose no one else has broken a neck or anything trivial?'

‘Two of the blackcocks are injured, sir.’

‘The *who*?’

‘Sorry, sir. I mean the Scots.’

‘What’s happened to them? Broken a wing or something?’ Pomona added sarcastically.

‘Precisely, sir. At least one of them. Fractured wrist, sir. Then there’s a suspected broken collar-bone. Don’t understand it quite myself, sir. Never been taken that way, flapping around like a lot of bloody roosters.’

‘Don’t worry. The way things are going there’s probably still time.’

‘I agree, sir. Rutting’s one thing but lekking’s quite another. I expect,’ the CSM added mysteriously, ‘it takes different people different ways.’

Pomona increasingly felt the need for a nice lie down. The disturbing thing was that beneath his bewilderment he was aware of a kind of understanding, sympathy even for what the CSM was saying. The singing in his ears had started again. He pulled himself together.

‘Is that all, Sergeant-Major?’

‘I’m afraid not. There’s that civilian bird person.’

‘Not Joanna Bromley?’

‘No, sir. None of the women are hurt. Some, I mean the ones who are “on”, have had a bit of going over already. They’re probably shagged, but on the whole they’re enjoying it. No, it’s Dr Mathews, sir. He turned up in the wrong rig, I mean plumage, so they did him.’

Pomona was obviously under the impression that Jerry Mathews had been giving another lekking lecture.

‘In my opinion, all these practical demonstrations have gone too far. They’ve got to stop.’

‘Quite, sir. No one needs lessons any more.’

‘Perhaps we’d better just concentrate on our real job here.’

‘That’s what I wanted to talk to you about, sir. With all these casualties, we’re very much below manning strength. And I’m afraid we must expect some more.’

‘We certainly must NOT, Sergeant-Major. I forbid it.’

‘It’s that civilian deer-watcher we’ve got to look out for.’

‘Dr Roxborough?’

‘Not him, sir. At present he doesn’t seem to know whether he’s the monarch of the glen or cock of the north . . . There are one or two like that. Sort of half and half. Probably like that in real life. But I expect they’ll get it sorted out. Look at Butch Cassidy and 007 Bond. As normal as you please suddenly.’

‘What, or who, the hell are you talking about then?’

‘Dr Hulke, sir. He’s on the loose, sir, and no one, not even you sir, can consider your life and limb safe until someone has settled with him.’

‘Thank you Sergeant-Major. That will be all for the moment. I want to see the revised manning rosters. And Sergeant-Major . . .’

‘Sir.’

‘I’m relying on you to see that there isn’t any more trouble.’

From long habit and training the CSM snapped up his smartest salute with his right hand. The CSM yelped with pain as his two broken ribs grated together.

‘Serve the bastard right for stirring it all up,’ Pomona thought. Then he reached for a message form and began to compose his SITREP.

October, second week

The Minister for Health positively purred at her PPS, a bland blond Etonian as willowy as a stalk of wheat and with ears to match. She was thinking what the latest report from Dundoom would do to that little squirt, Ted Illingworth, Minister for Energy.

'That's excellent news, Adrian. The Prime Minister must be told at once. You mean the symptoms are exclusively confined to this security man, Gilbey? Tried to assault three of them, you say?'

'One matron, one staff nurse and a hospital cook.'

'What on earth was the cook doing in an isolation ward?'

'It's not so much what the cook was doing in the ward as what Gilbey was doing to the cook in her own kitchen.'

'I gave orders he was to be under strict supervision, with a male nurse always on duty.'

'He knocked the chap out with a bed pan.'

'What about the women?'

'Didn't make first base with any of them apparently. The matron simply ordered him to get dressed and go back to bed before he caught his death.'

'You mean he was naked?'

'Starkers, Minister.'

'What about the staff nurse?'

'I gather she had been taking kung-fu classes and kicked him in a manner calculated to discourage.'

'Very parliamentarily put.'

'Thank you, Minister.'

'And *did* it discourage the poor chap?'

'Apparently not. Such was his state of . . . er . . . excitement that he rushed from the nurses' quarters straight to the kitchens where the cook, who was preparing cod pie at the time, hit him in the belly, or thereabouts, with a wet fish.'

'I've often heard the phrase,' said the Minister, 'but I

never expected to see the day when someone actually did it.'

'Most effective, I gather.'

'Where's the poor chap, now?'

'In a strait-jacket. Gilbey appears to be having a nervous breakdown, caused by sheer frustration. He can't understand why none of his victims wished to co-operate.'

'He must be extremely vain. Is he a very attractive man?'

'Utterly repulsive, I understand. Sort of human gorilla. A natural for a security guard. Probably couldn't get a job doing anything else.'

'Thank you, Adrian. That's very helpful. You'll give me a written minute within the next half-hour, please. The Prime Minister must have all the facts at once.'

Audrey Margetson felt a warm glow. She'd teach that little sod the Minister for Energy.

The Brigadier in command of Scottish tracking stations smoothed the message form that his staff captain had just handed him as if by doing so he could make the words disappear.

'What's this fellow Pomona like, Keith?'

'Excellent officer, sir. First rate technician, sir. You picked him yourself.'

'Doesn't seem to be a very good disciplinarian.' The Brigadier inspected Captain Pomona's SITREP more closely just in case he had missed something. He hadn't. He said slowly: 'One broken arm, one broken wrist, two broken ribs, one dislocated elbow, one other rank with suspected broken collar bone, one civilian badly concussed. It's impossible.'

'Perhaps they've been playing rugger, sir.'

'Don't be bloody silly, Keith. They've nowhere to play. Besides there aren't enough of them.'

'Training programme too strenuous, possibly, sir.'

'They're radar men, not the bloody SAS. Get me the Prime Minister's Private Secretary on the scrambler.'

When the call came through the Brigadier identified

himself and spoke the phrase he had been instructed to use if anything unusual was reported from Pomona. 'The Horn has blown,' he said.

'In that case,' said the PPS, 'the Prime Minister's instructions are to get round here immediately.'

Captain Bertram Pomona consulted his MO only in dire emergency. He had sought her advice – disastrously as he now realised by hindsight – when the over-reaching sexuality of his unit appeared to be adversely affecting its operational efficiency. Now he faced an even more serious crisis. With casualties among the masculine half of his force mounting almost hourly, he must consult her again.

A pleasant thought struck him. Lieutenant Preece would be off-duty now. He would call in to visit her on the way to Dr Whymper's quarters. After all, he told himself, she was an officer and a lady and quite an efficient example of at least the former. She would probably have her ear closer to the ground than the MO. Regina Whymper would be able to tell him the extent and nature of his casualties' injuries. Myfanwy Preece was more likely to have all the girl-talk, what the rude and licentious soldiery called latrine-rumours. He wondered what the feminine military equivalent was. Powder-room gossip, perhaps?

He knocked on Myfanwy's door. Normally, in her off-duty moments, he could rely on her being femininely if not actually tantalisingly dressed. Whenever he called she was apt to dispose herself about the furnishings in an arousing and seductive manner. She did this apparently naturally and without any deliberate coyness. But then it was hard not to display those legs in a totally destructive fashion. On more than one occasion, when there had been someone about in the corridor outside, Captain Pomona had been so overcome that he had to hurry out of the room. On others, when he was quite sure his presence hadn't been observed, equally compelling forces had driven him to hurry into it. Today he was in no danger. From the moment he opened the door he sensed that not only was Myfanwy Preece not in the mood for him but he was not in the mood for Myfanwy Preece. The air was filled with a quite appalling cheap scent. Myfanwy appeared to have sprayed herself with the stuff.

'God, Myfanwy. What is that muck? Disinfectant?'

'Something like that.'

She held up a bottle labelled 'Highland Heather'. 'My aunt sent it to me. Don't you think it's rather telling?'

'It's a knock-out,' Pomona said. 'Though God knows what it's meant to knock-out. Flies probably. What did you do with that Givenchy I gave you?' The Givenchy was a particular turn-on for Pomona.

'I lent it to Regina.'

'To *whom.*'

'Dear old Reggie.'

'I thought you hated her guts.'

'Not really. Not at the moment anyway. Haven't you noticed? We're all girls together suddenly.'

Come to think of it, Pomona had noticed, during the last few days there had certainly been an increasing tendency for the women to drift around in groups. They all seemed terribly palsy-walsy or anyway neutral towards each other. He hadn't heard half the usual bitchery that was the female counterpart of the male soldiers' moans.

'Besides,' Myfanwy went on, 'dear old Reggie has more need of the Givenchy than I have. For the next few days, anyway. Then I expect I shall come on.'

Pomona winced at the vulgarity of the expression. He wanted to say that as far as he was concerned, Myfanwy had never been off. But he felt no desire to pursue her using his undoubted gift for easy gallantry. He looked down at her legs in the hope that they would revive his flagging, no, his flagged enthusiasm. This time he felt something far stronger than disinterest. The sensation was closer to outright revulsion. The lovely Myfanwy sat with her legs well apart, her feet planted firmly beneath the table. It was a posture he had formerly associated with captains of ladies' golf teams and off-duty traffic wardens. Pomona was as much a sly looker-upper of women's skirts as the next man but this particular attitude was one he had found from youth to be as about as erotic as a low level view of a bishop's gaiters. The final shock took some time to penetrate. Myfanwy might just as well have covered those fabulous stems of hers in episcopal gaitering. In place of the usual shimmering nylon that encased the Lieutenant's underpinnings, thick lisle stockings totally obscured one of the finest views in the outer isles. The legs thus desecrated ended in flat-heeled brogues that did even less for Captain Pomona's limping libido.

On any other occasion, Myfanwy would have acknowledged the direction of Pomona's gaze with a simple feminine reflex action, such as affecting to pull her skirt down, sliding one calf against the other, massaging one ankle suggestively with its fellow. All she did now was to move her legs wider apart. The effect, even though it gave him an uninterrupted view of her underwear, was the biggest turn-off since the black-out of World War Two. The underwear itself completed the cooling process. Myfanwy was wearing the kind of elastic legged knickers which he had known since puberty as passion-killers.

'Cup of tea?' she invited.

'Er, no, thanks awfully. I was on my way to consult Reggie, actually. Professionally, I mean.'

'Good idea.' Myfanwy bit into a slice of buttered toast. Normally she made her suggestive most of eating anything. Now she merely chomped on this snack with the unambiguous efficiency of a mechanical crusher.

'I'll be getting along, then.'

'Good luck,' Myfanwy said, reaching for the strawberry jam. She added mysteriously: 'Watch out for Markham. He's pretending to have a broken rib.'

From the moment that Pomona knocked on the MO's door, he knew something was up. The very atmosphere was different. *Je Reviens* and stale nicotine had been replaced, or anyway overcome, by Givenchy. The MO wore a floral house-coat. It was not a particularly alluring garment and did little to disguise the outsize proportions of the woman it concealed. The effect was similar to that achieved by covering a Zeppelin with chintz curtains.

Regina Whymper did not speak. Instead she stood with submissively downcast eyes.

Pomona experienced a rush of strange and simultaneous

sensations. They included: a pawing action with the right foot which hurled the rug back against the door; a singing in the ears associated with an uncontrollable itching of the scalp; the compulsion to utter a strangled roar and an overwhelming desire to leap on the woman to escape from whom he would previously willingly have swum the Race of Horn on the ebb tide in a Force Eight gale.

For her part, Regina Whymper made one gesture of token resistance, placing a chair half-heartedly between Pomona and herself.

The captain gave another and more forceful grunting roar. Dr Whymper moved the chair aside and loosened her housecoat. Bertram Pomona lunged, sliding his hands under the garment and cupping those enormous breasts. As he did so he recalled briefly the immortal words of Corporal Gunnersbury overheard in a barrack room discussion on the relative merits of large and small mammalia. 'Any more than a handful,' Gunnersbury had opined, 'is pure waste.' The words flickered briefly across Captain Pomona's consciousness as past life is said to appear to a drowning man. The next second Pomona was indeed drowning, swept under and away beneath a tidal wave of woman.

As far as Pomona could remember afterwards, the experience had been neither particularly pleasant nor unpleasant, just compulsive and very short-lived. What he did recall was that he had to come up for a second and third time. After that he was definitely sunk. At the end of it all, she merely said: 'Close the door quietly when you go.'

'I doubt if I've got the strength to bang it,' Pomona told her.

When he limped away to his quarters, Myfanwy Preece was lounging outside in the corridor eating an apple.

'Okay?' She sounded only mildly interested.

Pomona fluttered his eyelids as if about to faint. Perhaps he *was* going to faint.

'Look out,' Myfanwy advised, 'Markham's not around but Hulke's probably lurking somewhere.'

He found Mavis Prendergast on duty in the orderly room.

'I wish to send an immediate signal to the MOD and mark it "urgent".'

When Captain Pomona handed her the message form she read it back carefully: 'Request permission to proceed on leave as soon as relief can be arranged.'

Mavis looked at him strangely. 'You wouldn't like me to delay this for a bit, sir? I mean: are you sure you want to leave right now? After all, sir, things have only just got started.'

'In that case,' Pomona told her, 'mark it "Priority One".'

The Brigadier had made his report.

'Well, now we know the worst,' said the Prime Minister, 'obviously Ted's gas has had a marked affect upon . . . what's this bloody island called?'

'Horn, sir,' supplied the Brigadier.

'Ah, but *do* we know the worst, Prime Minister?' Audrey Margetson demanded. 'We have a sort of casualty list but we've no way of knowing what lies behind those casualties.' The Minister for Health saw a chance of getting the Prime Minister on the run.

An assistant secretary poked his head round the door. He was holding a message form.

'This signal has just come from the Ministry of Defence.'

He was about to hand it to the Brigadier when the Prime Minister snatched it. The Prime Minister held the time-honoured view that anything except firing a gun was too delicate a matter to be left in the hands of the military.

'Good God,' said the Prime Minister. 'It's another signal from this chap Pomona. Has he gone nuts?'

'Without seeing the signal, sir,' the Brigadier said haughtily, 'I'm afraid I can't give you an opinion.'

'When his men are falling like flies, he's asking to be sent on leave – at once.'

'Might be a good idea,' the Minister for Energy suggested. 'Get him back here and find out just what is happening on Horn.'

'That,' said the Prime Minister, 'is about the most irresponsible suggestion I've heard in my entire and extensive career. No one, repeat no one, leaves that island. I want a *cordon sanitaire* thrown round it.'

'Very well, sir,' said the Brigadier, 'But we must maintain operational efficiency . . .'

'Would you describe the detachment on Horn as a vital bulwark of the West?'

As was well known, the Prime Minister was in favour of reducing Britain's armed forces even below their present pitiful strength.

'Hardly, sir. Naturally, it's backed up by other NATO tracking stations.'

'Then stand it down, man. We can't have a gang of violent radioactive incompetents telling us when World War Three is about to break out.'

'If something dreadful *has* happened on Horn,' Audrey Margetson suggested sweetly, 'we can't just expect it to go away by sealing the place off like a leper colony. Someone has got to go in there and find out what is going on.'

'A commando landing force.' The Brigadier brightened at the thought of action. 'Equipped with Geiger counters. Just as if there's been a real nuclear attack.'

'What do you mean "just as if" . . . ' The Minister for Health nodded towards Ted Illingworth. 'There has been a nuclear attack . . . by our own side . . .'

'In that case,' said the Brigadier, 'we should mount a full-scale operation. It can be part of the NATO naval exercises due to take place off north-west Scotland. We'll move in in battalion strength, hold the beach-head while special units swan inland to assess the scale of nuclear damage.'

'When you've all quite finished playing soldiers,' the Prime Minister said frostily, 'I will tell you exactly what we will do. To start with I'm not having a lot of big-booted marines stomping all over the island creating panic. What I require is a discreet scientific investigation conducted in the utmost secrecy.'

'May I suggest, Prime Minister, a team of nuclear experts from the Ministry of Energy.'

'I don't want your chaps doing a snow-job on Horn.' The Prime Minister was rather proud of the jargon he had acquired during a recent visit to Washington. 'Tell your fellows to clear up their own mess at Dundoom. Find out exactly what it was they let loose the other night. And how to counter it.'

'This investigation is obviously a job for the Ministry of Health. If radiation is the danger, then we need a specialist on genetics, hormones . . .'

'Send me the name of your genetics specialist within the hour, Audrey.'

'Maybe I should go myself.'

'I need you here.' The last thing the Prime Minister desired was the Minister for Health blowing her own trumpet on Horn.

'I really think you'll need a first-class nuclear warfare man, sir. An expert to estimate the degree and permanence of the radiation.'

'Good point, Brigadier. I'll have your nomination, too, within the hour, please. But bear in mind, the mission is to be extremely low-profile. No panic. It must look like a routine Government visit of inspection. Certainly no uniforms. What do your fellows wear when they're in mufti, Brigadier?'

'Bowler hats and rolled umbrellas, sir.'

'Excellent. Decidedly low-profile.'

Ted Illingworth said: 'I feel we need a highly responsible scientist to head the mission. I can make a suggestion from my own department.'

'NERTS,' said Audrey Margetson with feeling.

The Prime Minister wasn't going to be caught by this gag a second time. 'This is not the moment for levity, Audrey.'

'I wasn't being facetious. At least, not very. I suddenly thought of Sir Irwin Broadchalke, the head NERT. After all, he *is* a scientist. His people *are* on the island. What's most important, he always wears a bowler hat.'

'Definitely low-profile,' agreed the Prime Minister. 'Excellent idea.'

'How soon can we get them in, Brigadier?'

'As soon as they're briefed, say in eight hours. We can chopper them in.'

'Good, but the chopper is to leave immediately they've been put down. Now,' said the Prime Minister, feeling better at having made a few decisions, 'we'll start composing some signals to – what's this fellow called?'

'Pomona, sir.'

'Exactly. Damn funny name for a British Army Officer. Sure he's reliable?'

Captain Pomona viewed the signal that Mavis Prendergast handed him next morning with puzzlement and displeasure. He had a sore throat which added to his feeling of general ill-being. Or, if not exactly a sore throat, a kind of roughness of the larynx which had somehow made his voice sound deeper. Strangely enough, he had noticed the same tendency in CSM Markham and Corporal Gunnersbury. Must be infectious, whatever it was. Perhaps the MO would have something for it. The thought of Dr Whymper set him quivering. Shattered as he was by yesterday's extraordinary experience, he still felt drawn to her. He should have been terrified at the thought of having to go through all that again. Part of him even wondered whether he would survive a second session.

He cleared his throat. Goddam it, he sounded like a bass baritone. 'When did this signal come in?'

'At 0700 hrs. this morning, sir,' Mavis Prendergast told him.

He read it over a second time.

'No leave will be granted to personnel of your unit until further notice. This applies to all ranks. Owing to casualties as reported by you, manning watch will be stood down effective as from receipt this signal. O/C Horn to devise comprehensive training programme to occupy all ranks. Acknowledge immediately.'

Pomona's already aching head spun. The radar station on Horn, he had always been given to understand, was a key part of the West's early warning system. Surely they could send him a few replacements to keep him up to strength. As for a training programme! What the hell kind of training programme? Not another round of rutting and lekking lectures with Scottish dancing thrown in as an encore. God forbid! He'd been all through that once, and look where it had got them all. Could the Brigadier mean dummy runs with the tracking equipment? If so, he needed more than a red band round his cap to hold his brains together. The unit had been tracking real satellites, monitoring practice missiles and following migrating bird flocks for months. He looked up suddenly. Lieutenant Preece stood in front of his desk, saluting smartly.

'Good morning, sir.'

Pomona regarded Myfanwy Preece without particular interest. After yesterday's performance, she was slightly less intriguing than the latest amendment to Queen's Regs.

The Lieutenant cut away her salute with dash and elan.

'Good morning, sir.' Very formal.

'Good morning, Lieutenant.'

'I have a request to make, sir. It's about a training programme for my girls.'

'Oh.' Pomona brightened. He'd often heard that the Welsh had second sight. How could Myfanwy have guessed that this was just what the MOD had ordered?

'They need to become more self-sufficient. They need hardening up.'

Pomona privately doubted whether this was what they did need. Softness, he had always thought, was one of their most useful military characteristics.

'So what do you suggest?'

'It's not entirely my suggestion, sir. The girls themselves put the idea forward. They want to have a spell under canvas.'

Pomona let this information seep slowly into his consciousness. 'You do realise,' he said at last, 'that we're into October. The nights are quite frosty.'

'We'll issue winter clothing. We'll keep warm somehow.'

'I bet,' thought Pomona. Aloud he asked: 'Where do you plan to camp out?'

'You know that nice heathery slope above the shearing shed?'

'Good Lord, Myfanwy. That's damn miles away.'

'Don't worry sir. I'll arrange for the manning detail to be transported back and forth, of course.'

'Sit down, Myfanwy. I have the most extraordinary news for you. We've been stood down, or perhaps up.'

Myfanwy scanned the signal rapidly.

'That's great.'

'I'm glad you see it that way. The Brigadier can't think much of us.'

Myfanwy ignored the implied disgrace. 'I don't really see that we could go on manning the station with all the fellers bashing each other about. Do I have your permission to go ahead immediately?'

'I suppose so, Myfanwy. At least it'll keep the girls out of mischief.' Pomona sincerely doubted this. 'What about the men?'

'I think you'll find they want their own kind of toughening up course, living out on the hill, so to speak.'

'Well, they'd better keep clear of your tent lines.'

'That's *their* problem,' said Myfanwy darkly.

October, third week

Soon after breakfast next morning Janet Morgan visited Graham MacCallister. This in itself was unusual. Though they had seen far more of each other since the night of the Highland dancing, it had previously always been Graham who casually dropped into Janet's laboratory.

'Morning, Graham.'

'Good morning, Janet.'

'How's Jerry? Has he got over his concussion or whatever it was?'

'Must have done. He's sugared off.'

Janet frowned slightly at the phrase.

'What's that supposed to mean, exactly?'

'Scarpered. Split. Vamoosed.' Graham thought she looked even more delightful when she was annoyed, so he added, 'taken a powder. Taken his pup tent and outdoor gear with him, too.'

'That's funny, Joanna's gone as well.'

'There's nothing strange in that. They've always been great ones for communal nature study.'

'I know all about that, Graham. But they haven't gone together. Joanna's taken the stuff she uses when she's camping on Hummel to watch gannets.'

'The gannets aren't there at this time of the year.'

'I know that, you idiot . . .'

Graham glowed with pleasure. It was the first time Janet had ever used such an endearment.

'She said something about camping out with the Army girls,' Janet continued. 'Apparently they're on a kind of training exercise to toughen them up.'

'Hardly seems necessary from what I've seen of them. I hope they've got their drawers, thermal, privates for the protection of. It's going to be damn nippy from now on.'

'I say, Graham.'

'Yes.'

'Do you feel that everything's rather strange suddenly?'

It was only a few days since Graham had asked her the same sort of question.

'I suppose so. Jerry bashed up in that extraordinary fashion. And Fergus . . . where is Fergus by the way?'

'Exactly. All dressed up in a kilt and wearing that absurd sporran all the time. Besides, he practically never shows up here.'

'Hulke *never* shows up. At least not for the last couple of days. Not that I'm sorry about that.'

'I even had to get my own breakfast this morning.'

'So did I. Where *is* Flora?'

Janet giggled deliciously. 'Sugared off,' she said. 'Scarpered. Vamoosed. Split. Taken a powder.'

Graham regarded her gravely.

'Sit down, Janet,' he said carefully. 'I'm beginning to think you're right. Something rather unusual is happening to us all. You sure *you're* feeling all right?'

'On and off, I do feel rather odd, Graham.'

'That's good then.'

'What's that supposed to mean?'

Before Graham could reply, the air was torn by a hoarse roaring. On a rock above the tiny harbour stood CSM Markham, one arm clamped to his side to protect his damaged ribs, the other holding to his lips a loud-hailer, borrowed from the equipment store. With the aid of this he was filling the air with a raucous bellowing.

'Good God,' said Graham. 'He sounds just like a bloody stag.'

The Prime Minister regarded the names submitted to him with suspicion.

'You're certain they're secure.'

'Absolutely, sir,' his private secretary assured him. 'Sir Irwin's a top government scientist, of course.'

'So were Fuchs and Pontecorvo from what I recall. What about the nuclear chap?'

'Regular Army Colonel, name of Snettisham. Sniffy Snettisham, I believe he's known as.'

'That should guarantee unflappability.'

The private secretary could never be quite sure when his chief was being sarcastic. So he acted on the assumption that unless the Prime Minister had thought of an idea or nominated a person himself, he was being sarcastic. Using this rule of thumb he was right, at least ninety per cent of the time.

'What about the doctor?'

'Very bright chap from Guy's. Lucrative Harley Street practice. Said to be the No. 1 man where hormonal balance and genetic influences of radiation are concerned. Observer at several atomic tests and highly thought of by NASA. Name of Braithwaite, Raymond Braithwaite. Aged forty-two. No Communist affiliations, even in student days.'

'What does he vote?'

'For the other lot, I'm afraid, sir. But then that has advantages, sir. If the mission does well we can afford to look generous. If they make a booboo of it . . .'

'I don't like the phrase. Quite apart from that, we can't even contemplate making a booboo of this. If anything *has* happened on that bloody island it's got to be handled very delicately.'

'Quite, sir. No doubt you'll make that point very forcibly in your personal briefing.'

'What about the bowler hats and, I suggest, rolled umbrellas?'

'Been issued, sir. Of course, Broadchalke and the army chap had their own. Apparently Dr Braithwaite runs more to trilbies and check caps. Drives a Jensen.'

'He can probably afford to, but we can't have any of that sort of carry-on on Horn. Got to keep a low profile.'

'I've already explained that, sir.'

'How did he take it?'

'Rather well, sir. Said he wished he'd worn a bowler before, might have enabled him to put his fees up.'

'I doubt it,' said the Prime Minister. 'I expect he earns enough to finance the Health Service already. By the way: what *are* we paying him?'

'Nothing, sir. Dr Braithwaite said he regarded it as an honour.'

'Damned doctors,' said the Prime Minister. 'I'll never

understand them. Always complaining about being overworked and underpaid and then do a job like this for damn-all.'

'I expect that's because we'd only take it all away in tax, anyway.'

'You may be right. Anyway, I'd better see them all. I suppose someone's told them it might be dangerous.'

'At the briefing, Dr Braithwaite said he'd always fancied changing his sex.'

'I suppose he's not queer,' the Prime Minister said anxiously.

Pomona poured himself a large Scotch and prepared to relax. The stresses of the last few days had been rather too much. Even the organisation of Myfanwy's survival course had proved something of a hassle. At the last minute, the Scots girls had asked whether they could be allowed to set up a separate camp on what he understood to be a blackcock lekking ground. Lieutenant Preece had emphasised that she would, of course, be in charge of the outdoor training programmes at both camps which would be known respectively as Blackcock and Hind.

The disposal of the male members of his unit released from manning duty had been simpler. The walking wounded, Corporal Gunnersbury and Lance-Corporal Mason, were to remain at HQ as cook and orderly room clerk respectively. CSM Markham, with ribs encased in Elastoplast, had volunteered to take out daily parties on hill walks and infantry training.

To Pomona's great relief, Dr Whymper had said she felt most strongly that her place was with the girls in the field.

Lance-Corporal Mason entered the orderly room and saluted with his left hand. Was it his imagination or had Mason's voice dropped a couple of octaves?

'You'll have to excuse me saluting all arsy-tarsy, sir. My right antler's broken.'

'Your *what*?'

'Sorry, sir. Couldn't have been thinking, sir. My right elbow's damaged, sir.'

'You got a sore throat, Lance-Corporal?'

'Well, now you come to mention it, sir, my throat has gone sort of gruff. How about yours, sir?'

Pomona cleared his throat. 'Not at all, Mason.' As he said this he was aware that he sounded as though he was gurgling with half a pound of granite chips.

'Mind you,' said Mason. 'The moment my throat started acting up, my scalp stopped itching.'

'What the hell has that got to do with it?'

'Probably nothing, sir. Just thought I'd mention it. Singing in the ears has stopped, too.'

'That's funny,' said Pomona before he could check himself, 'so's mine.'

'There you are then, sir.'

'Very likely, Mason.'

'Though you don't have a broken antler, sir.'

'What the hell is this conversation about?' Pomona demanded irritably. 'Neither of us has antlers.'

'CSM Markham used a chair. Much the same effect as antlers, sir.'

Pomona chose to ignore this.

'What did you come to see me about?'

'A signal, sir.'

'Good Lord, man. Then why didn't you produce it at once?'

'Sorry, sir, you seemed to want to know about my voice, sir, and, of course, my damaged antler . . . I mean elbow, sir.'

'Well let's have the signal. Who's it from?'

'MOD sir, marked urgent.'

Captain Pomona took the message form and read.

'Expect helicopter to deliver routine repeat routine MOD and NERT inspection team 1200 hrs. tomorrow. Team consists of Sir Irwin Broadchalke, head NERT, Colonel Snettisham MOD, Dr Raymond Braithwaite medical officer of health. Arrange accommodation but otherwise continue routine training programme as ordered in recent signal. Signed Brigadier i/c Radar Tracking Units, Scotland.'

About two hours before the MOD chopper was due to

touch down with its bowler-hatted commando force, Graham MacCallister made an amazing discovery. One of the facets of his deer faeces study was to analyse a random collection of droppings each week for signs of pollution, airborne DDT, the effects of excessive carbon monoxide, diesel fumes in the atmosphere, and general environmental nastiness. Graham made the tests regularly and conscientiously, though in a state of numbed boredom. In the pure and bracing air of Horn he thought it extremely unlikely that any of its herd of 200 red deer would suffer from the sort of pollutive complaints that were part of the daily lives of, say, the citizens of Los Angeles or even Wigan. Once a week he was also required to screen a series of selected deer pellets for the effects of abnormal radiation. To make this test he was equipped with a miniature but highly specialised Geiger counter. To date this instrument had not produced a single sinister click.

He laid his specimen dung out on the bench, ranging it by the altitude at which it had been collected from right to left. The right hand pellet had been picked up just below the Tine at 2800 feet two days ago. The dropping on the extreme left had come from the low ground by the Army's main tracking aerial a day later.

He switched on the counter and held it over the high altitude dung. To his amazement the instrument emitted a series of faint clicks spaced at intervals of fifteen seconds. To teach it a lesson he banged the instrument hard against the edge of the table. Obstinately, the machine repeated its performance. Specimen number two had been picked up at 2500 feet on the same day. The clicks were there again, though this time the interval between them was minimally shorter. He hurried on to the pellet next in descending order. The clicks were both louder and faster. Now, fascinated by the experiment, he carried on down the line. For the 1000 feet pellet the signal was much louder and extremely frequent. By the time he reached the lowest specimen of all, the miniature Geiger counter was beating a regular tattoo.

The instrument was so sensitive that it registered minute amounts of abnormal radiation. There was no doubt in

Graham's mind that it was indicating an event far beyond the norm. Delighted that his study had at last revealed something more exciting than the time taken by a stem of bog cotton to pass through a three-year-old hind's gut, he rushed into Janet's workroom.

'We're radioactive,' he announced.

'Graham, do express yourself more clearly.'

'The faecal pellets. They're all clicking away like castanets.'

It was a tribute to Janet's limpidly clear mind that she was able to connect the word 'radioactive' with 'castanets' and come up with the right answer – 'Geiger counter'.

So Graham repeated the experiment for her. He did so with the pride of an amateur conjuror who has purchased a ready-made trick and can perform it, but hasn't the faintest idea how it works.

'What do you make of it, Janet?'

'The interesting thing is that the signs of radioactivity increase in almost direct proportion to the decrease in altitude.'

'Maybe the Russians have let off an atomic bomb somewhere.'

'Or the Americans. I don't see why you should always assume it's the Russians.' It was typical of Janet to try to be fair to all.

'When do you suppose it happened?'

'Well, we can get some idea of that from the pellets. You did your last tests for radioactivity a week ago today?'

'Yes.'

'The oldest dropping is two days old?'

'Two and a half days at least.'

'How long does vegetation take to pass through a deer's digestive system?'

'Between six and sixteen hours.'

'Fine. So the island got its dose of whatever it was not more than seven days ago and not less than three.'

'Janet.'

'Yes.'

'When did you start complaining of feeling a bit queer? Singing in the ears and that kind of thing.'

'About three days ago.'

'Same with me.'

'Graham, do you remember anything unusual about that time?'

'The Army held its dance that night.'

'And we went out on the hill under the full moon.'

'I don't see what that has to do with it.'

'Nor do I. I'm just trying to pin-down the time when the island – and presumably ourselves – got this extra dose of radiation.'

'Maybe it's nothing worth worrying about. This apparatus of mine is pretty sensitive.'

'We should at least report your findings.'

'Who to?'

'It should be Fergus. After all, he's the head of the scientific mission.'

'He's behaving far too eccentrically to be the head of anything. As far as I can make out he's dashing off into the heather at all hours dressed like Bonnie Prince Charlie.'

'Perhaps,' Janet said gravely, 'we should at least alert the military. Captain Pomona ought to know.'

'I think you were right the first time. Fergus, after all, is a scientist. He's not so liable to flap . . .'

The loud honking of a klaxon horn interrupted this sentence. Through the window they glimped Dr Fergus Roxborough running in obvious panic up the village track, sporran askew, plaid flying in the wind. Twice he looked back in terror over his shoulder. Behind him, at full throttle, bouncing and prancing over the rocks, rearing up on its back wheel like a mettlesome horse, leaping an obstruction with both wheels clear of the ground, hurtled the Greaves scrambler. A wild-eyed MacGregor stood upright in the saddle. As he passed he yelled: 'I'll show ye whether ye're a blackcock or a bluidy stag.'

Fergus Roxborough leapt, at the very last moment, into the heather. MacGregor skidded to a halt. Then he gunned his engine and roared up on to the crag above the little harbour where CSM Markham had previously given his extraordinary display with the loud-hailer.

MacGregor sat triumphant in his saddle. The Greaves' upswept handlebars were silhouetted against the sky. Then he began to roar away with his klaxon. From some distance, CSM Markham replied with a bellow over the loud-hailer. Hardly had his last roar died away, than a third and even more faraway sound echoed across the heather. Far off someone was blowing a bugle on a cracked and hysterical note.

Dr Janet Morgan hadn't been trained as an animal behaviourist for nothing.

'They're all behaving' she said, with total accuracy, 'like a lot of belling stags.'

Early that morning Captain Pomona decided he would see how the girls were getting on under canvas. To say that *he* had decided would be putting it too strongly. In fact he had a distinct aversion to hiking nearly two miles over rock and heather to watch Myfanwy's girls boil an egg by rubbing two sticks together.

It was greatly to the credit of Bertram Pomona's training and background as a professional soldier that, despite these blind and imperative urges, he still retained some of the qualities of command. At least within the confines of his own orderly room he remained in charge of himself.

'Lance-Corporal Mason.'

'Sir.'

'You've made all the necessary arrangements to accommodate Colonel Snettisham and these two civilian gentlemen when they arrive?'

'Yes, sir. I've billetted them all up at the spare NERTS cottage.'

'Excellent. Don't want them messing about round here. Besides, I thought I might go out and join the troops under canvas myself.'

'Some guys have all the luck.'

'I beg your pardon, Mason.'

'I mean, I'd like to be out in the field myself.'

'I'm sure it could be arranged.'

'Perhaps not, sir. I couldn't risk meeting the CSM again.

Not now he's shown his dominance. I'd just have to see him going into his parallel walk and I'd run like a stag, I mean a staggie.'

'Just what the hell are you talking about?'

'The parallel walk, sir. That Dr Roxborough told us about it in his rutting lecture. It's a sort of routine that Company Sergeant-Majors, I mean master stags, go into before they put their antlers, I mean their chairs, down and charge the hell out of poor wee staggies like me. It's how I got my elbow buggered.'

Pomona found that, muddled as Mason's explanation was, he seemed to catch the drift of it all.

'Lance-Corporal, I can quite appreciate how you feel. However, I must make quite clear that CSM Markham's parallel walk will cut no ice with me. After all he's been horned, I mean chaired, in the ribs himself.'

'Good luck, then, sir. But mind that Dr Hulke. He's the one you've got to look out for, all right.'

Sir Irwin Broadchalke, Colonel Sniffy Snettisham and Dr Raymond Braithwaite watched the sunlit October sea glint beneath the helicopter's rotors with a variety of feelings. Three bowler hats and an equal number of rolled umbrellas lay in the luggage racks above their heads. Sir Irwin, who had a taste for eccentricity, had cheerfully complied with the Prime Minister's request to keep their mission low-profile. He had decided to wear sponge-bag trousers and a black jacket. Colonel Snettisham had opted for a conventional off-duty pin-stripe while the doctor had compromised with a sporty Savile Row tweed that gave him the air of a Newmarket trainer.

The civilian pilot of the chartered chopper pointed ahead.

'Hummel coming up on the horizon to port. The peak you can see beyond is Ben Dhui. It's Horn's mini Matterhorn.'

Sniffy Snettisham pointed to four or five V-shaped wakes far off to port.

'Rather a lot of shipping in these parts, isn't there?'

'There's some sort of NATO exercise just starting. I hope

they know we're coming otherwise we'll probably get buzzed by some Biggles in a Harrier.'

Ten minutes later Hummel, separated by a raging tidal race of white water from Horn, was so close it seemed you could reach out and touch the ledges where the gannets nested in spring and summer. The pilot lost altitude, banking round the cliffs to give his passengers a gannet's eye view. Sir Irwin, who felt distinctly uneasy except when sitting in a vertical position, stared down distastefully at the viscous green moil of the sea around the base of the granite cliffs. How nasty it would be, he thought, to fall in there. He tried hard to concentrate on the mission that lay ahead.

'Your task,' the Prime Minister had said, 'is to find out not only whether Ted Illingworth's blasted leak reached this pestilential island, but what affect, if any, it has had, or is likely to have, on the personnel stationed there. Weather permitting, the chopper will come back whenever you call up on the radio. I want a personal report within twelve hours of your returning to the mainland. Meantime there's a total security black-out. Good luck.'

'Good luck,' Sir Irwin repeated to himself as the pilot, now thoroughly enjoying himself, made a pass along the sheer nesting cliffs at sea level and a rotor's breadth from the rock.

'That's quite enough of that,' Sir Irwin commanded with what resolution he had left. 'We'll proceed to Horn now.'

'Okay, squire,' the pilot told him cheerfully. 'Where do you want me to put you down?'

Sir Irwin hadn't thought about this. It was extremely unlikely that the Army had a helipad. On the other hand, they must own a parade ground. Or should they drop in, as it were, first on the NERTS? After all, he was the head NERT.

'Better take a look around first,' he told the pilot. 'Fly straight and level please. We want to get the lie of the land.'

'Gotja squire,' the pilot said. At that moment he was threatening to dip his landing gear in the whitecapped crests of the Race. The cliffs of Horn approached alarmingly fast. At the last moment, the helicopter shot up over the top with the erratic ease of a dragon-fly.

Colonel Snettisham reached for his bowler hat. Now that the enemy coast was coming up, so to speak, it was time to be putting on one's equipment.

They came in over the Tracking Unit's little group of huts. The pilot circled twice without anyone spotting a sign of life.

'Looks like the *Marie Celeste,*' he volunteered.

Sir Irwin ignored this. 'Carry on up the east coast to the settlement' he instructed.

'As you say, squire.' This mode of address was beginning to irk Sir Irwin.

'I am not a squire. I am, in fact, a knight.'

The pilot's answer to this sally was to descend to wave-top height again in order to enter the narrow entrance of the harbour between the piles of granite that formed its twin jetties and then to zoom up over the cottages at maximum power. He was rewarded by hearing Sir Irwin behind him swallowing hard. When they came round in a reasonably gentle bank for the second time, two figures were standing outside one of the cottages. Sir Irwin recognised Janet and the young man he had selected to study faecal pellets.

The helicopter climbed away and headed inland. Almost at once, Sniffy Snettisham announced: 'There's a camp up ahead.' They flew on for thirty seconds before the Colonel added: 'Good God! They've all gone mad. They're dancing.'

'It's a very strange sort of dance,' Sir Irwin said. 'Fellers in kilts darting around. Looks more like they're having a scrap.'

'There's a girl,' Dr Braithwaite announced with interest. 'I say. She's dragging one of the chaps off.'

The pilot made a low, slow pass over a couple, who oblivious to the downwash of the rotor, were inextricably entwined in the grass.

'If that's dancing,' said the pilot,' I don't know my *passo doble* from my military two-step.'

As they gained altitude, Sniffy Snettisham shouted:

'Hey, wait a minute. There's another lot of tents higher up in the heather.'

Captain Pomona surveyed the scene before him.

Myfanwy Preece's camp was well laid out, the tents in two groups inconspicuously sited in gullies in the heather. A burn ran close by and a fire glowed in the grate of a cooking stove cunningly fashioned from turf and boulders. From a military point of view the lay-out was beyond criticism. It was the activity surrounding the tents that baffled Captain Pomona.

On a rock above the larger group of tents stood, or rather loomed, his company sergeant-major. Every so often the CSM threw back his head and gave a wild bellow, amplified at the least to the power of ten by means of a loud-hailer. Outside the tents, Lieutenant Preece was attempting to conduct some sort of parade with a gaggle of female soldiers. It was only too obvious that her class was distracted, even fascinated, by Markham's roarings. Just then, Pomona spotted another figure lurking on the outskirts of the huddle of tents. Lurk was the only word to describe the furtive movements of Dr Fergus Roxborough.

As Pomona watched, CSM Markham descended from his commanding position and charged down upon the group, seizing the lesbian cook, Butch Cassidy, and dragging her away without visible signs of outrage towards the nearest two-man, or possibly one-woman one-man, tent. None of the other lady soldiers reacted in the slightest to this remarkable abduction. Not so Fergus Roxborough who immediately moved in at a smart trot and began to nuzzle the neck of the other cook, Hideous 007 Bond.

Cassidy and Bond, thought Pomona. A fate that only a few days ago would have seemed as unlikely and far more hideous to both the CSM and the head of NERT than castration with a rusty bayonet. What had happened to make those two suddenly attractive to normal heterosexual males? As if the answer, Captain Pomona experienced an over-powering urge to join in. He began to run towards the scene of the action. As he did so, the chopper appeared round the shoulder of Ben Dhui. He ignored it and galloped on.

'Seems to be a spot of activity down below,' the pilot announced. 'I could put you down there, squire.'

'Good, good!' said Irwin. 'And be quick about it, please.'

'No sooner said than done.' The pilot slid the chopper into a horrifying downward swoop that came within a swallow of outwitting Sir Irwin's stomach at the very last moment.

The downwash from the rotor sucked up and whisked away the tent into which Roxborough and Hideous 007 Bond had recently disappeared.

'Blind O'Reilly,' said the pilot when he saw what was revealed. 'Any chance of signing up in your army? Who's the geyser in the kilt? Never realised before just how handy they could be. No doubt what he doesn't wear under his.'

'It's Roxborough.' Such was the shock at finding his chief of mission in *flagrante delicto* that Sir Irwin forgot that his stomach was still two hundred feet above him.

Colonel Snettisham reached for his umbrella. The assault was about to go in. 'Looks to me,' he announced, 'as if this radioactivity has done something very serious to the discipline of this unit.'

'Whatever else it's done,' the doctor sounded jubilant at the prospects ahead, 'it doesn't seem to have dented their libido.'

'Low-profile, gentlemen.' Sir Irwin felt it incumbent on him as the senior man present to re-emphasise the Prime Minister's orders. He put on his own bowler hat and glared at the doctor to do likewise.

'Would it be all right if I just carried mine? Not really my style, a bowler.'

'The Prime Minister's instructions were very explicit.'

The helicopter sat gently down in the heather.

'Mind the rotors when you hop out,' the pilot told them good-naturedly, 'or you won't have anything left to put your bowler hats on.'

'You're to take off at once,' Sir Irwin instructed.

'Suits me, squire. Though I wouldn't mind a slice of what seems to be available first.'

'At once!'

'Okay, squire. Keep your bowler on. When do I pick you up?'

'Your firm will receive a signal about that in due course.'

The pilot slid open the cabin door.

'Okay, troops,' he said, 'over the top and the best of British.'

Captain Pomona increased his canter. He did not know what his exact intentions were but he knew he was going to be a hard man to stop. He was dimly aware that the possessive behaviour exhibited by both Markham and Roxborough had triggered off in him feelings of extreme aggression. As he galloped on towards the descending helicopter he was conscious of the group of women watching him in a curiously docile yet interested way, as if waiting to see what would develop.

Three figures, dressed as if for a stroll down St James's Street had jumped down from the chopper.

Hardly pausing to adjust his dress before leaving, CSM Markham bore down on Fergus Roxborough, catching him a shattering blow on the shoulder that sent him staggering knee-deep into the burn. By the time Roxborough had waded to the far bank, Markham had leapt the stream higher up and begun chasing him up the braeside. This left the field open to Pomona.

The three city gents now stood between Pomona and the women. Pomona knew that he meant to round up as many of these apparently receptive ladies as his strength would allow. But now three bowler-hatted newcomers stood in his way. He put his head down and, at full throttle, butted Sniffy Snettisham in the midriff. Sniffy's last thought as the breath was driven out of his lungs was that he, a full Colonel in recognisably off-duty civilians, had been assaulted by a mere Captain in uniform. This would mean a court martial. Where was Sir Irwin with his low-profile approach now? On his arse, if he didn't look out. The Colonel's head struck a rock and he passed out cold.

Swerving left-handed round the fallen Colonel, Pomona headed for Sir Irwin who, with commendably fast reactions, put his head down to receive the oncoming charge. Perhaps the thought occurred to him in those few crucial seconds that the bowler had originally been designed as a sort of upper-crust crash helmet to protect the head on the hunting field. The Broadchalkes were, after all, a family well connected in the shires. They knew about such things.

Captain Pomona's skull met Mr Lock's prime headgear squarely on the dome and crunched it over Sir Irwin's ears and, indeed, eyes with the force of a kick from the rear end of a sixteen hand heavyweight hunter. Sir Irwin staggered to the blow, commendably stayed on his feet and then tottered around helplessly in the heather, totally blindfolded by the leather band inside the concertinaed bowler. He was out of the fight.

The group of females edged nervously nearer to Pomona whose eye now fell on Cecilia Munt. He had never in his furthest-out fantasies fancied the gangling Cecilia. But now he desired nothing more strongly than to separate her from the rest and drag her off as Markham and Roxborough had dragged off the cooks. First, however, there was the third city gent to be dealt with.

Dr Raymond Braithwaite prepared to defend himself. Holding his obligatory bowler as a shield in his left hand, he took up the on-guard position, umbrella poised like an épée in his right. He had been Under-Sixteen fencing champion at his public school. He was not going to let the old college down now.

Pomona came from an officer's training school where they had been taught to fight dirty with pick handles and other blunt instruments. It was thus a contest of broadsword against rapier.

Snatching up Sir Irwin's fallen umbrella by the pointed end he came on, swinging. At the first wild swipe he succeeded in opening up the crown of the doctor's hat as if taking the top off a lightly boiled egg. His next swing caught the doctor's umbrella and hurled it far out into the heather. Friar Tuck could not have done better. The doctor turned to run but Captain Pomona hooked his legs from under him with the umbrella handle.

From a hundred feet above the arena, the chopper pilot viewed these battles with delighted amazement. What a bunch of weirdos! Screwing and fighting. They were two activities that touched the romantic streak in his Mach One soul. He had half a mind to land and join in. Orders were orders, though. Even more to the point, there were a lot of good chopper pilots bucking for jobs since the oil business came to Scotland. Better to play it safe. Still, what a story he'd have to tell when he got back to the mainland. He made another circuit of the battlefield.

Pomona moved in on Cecilia Munt. Why her? Undoubtedly because she was 'on', whatever that signified. So, he was certain, was Mavis Prendergast. She'd have to wait her turn and, from the doe-eyes she was making, seemed quite willing to do so. He closed on Private Munt.

From on high the chopper pilot saw the new arrival long before any one else. A great burly, tweedy figure came bursting round a bend in the burn, throwing up clouds of spray as he careered madly forward, for all the world like a stag galloping up a stream to confuse those following his scent. Except that this stag was not confusing a scent but following one.

Pomona spotted the newcomer far too late. Cecilia and Mavis had already started to run back in submissive panic to join the herd of women. Pomona felt himself gripped in a wrestler's hold and hurled, hooves over antlers, into the burn.

Triumphant, Dr Hammond Hulke stood on a rock and roared louder even than CSM Markham had done with the aid of the loud hailer. Then, leaving the fallen on the field, Dr Hulke rounded up all the women and drove them before him high up into the heather.

'Christ!' said the chopper pilot to himself. 'Nobody told me about him. Like a bloody wild beast. No thanks. I'm heading home.'

And he did so, wondering as he set course for the mainland, whether anyone would believe his story.

*

When Graham MacCallister, attracted by the gyrations of the helicopter, arrived on the scene, the encampment resembled the aftermath of the Battle of Wounded Knee, except that the squaws had escaped intact, well hardly that perhaps, while the corpses on the field were all those of fallen braves. Only Pomona was missing. Having removed as much of the burn water from his clothing and person as a few good shakes would allow, he had decided to inspect his late opponents. The first body he came across was that of Colonel Snettisham. The face was familiar. So was that neat suit and REME tie. With cold horror Pomona realised where he had met Sniffy Snettisham before. The Colonel had given a Staff College lecture which Pomona had attended on 'Nuclear Attack and its After-Effects'.

The attack on his senior officer had been anything but nuclear. It had been extremely personal. The after-effects were only too evident, a badly contused temple and a grade one case of concussion. Pomona's military background briefly reasserted itself. It was possible, in view of the *blitzkrieg* nature of the assault, that Colonel Snettisham hadn't had time to recognise his assailant. Even so, a strategic withdrawal was called for before the Colonel came round. Captain Pomona withdrew.

Graham's first action was to make sure that both Braithwaite and the Colonel were still breathing. Next he retrieved the sightless figure of the third victim from the edge of a minor precipice over which it was about to totter.

'Help! Help!' pleaded Sir Irwin piteously. 'That maniac has blinded me.'

'You're quite okay,' Graham tried to sound reassuring. 'You'll be able to see in a minute.'

'I'm afraid not. It's quite extraordinary. All I have is a retinal image of the word LOCK. In gold letters, too.'

'Sit down on the rock. Now hold on. This may hurt a bit.'

Graham applied considerable leverage to all that remained of Mr Lock's bowler hat. That distinguished hatter would have been proud of the struggle that his elegant creation put up without offering to budge by so much as a centimetre.

'Bloody tight fit.'

'You're not another homicidal maniac are you? Mother of God, it will be my ears next. The Prime Minister never told me it would turn you all into murderers.'

Graham was too exhausted by the tug-of-war with the ruined bowler to ask what this meant, so he said: 'Sit still and keep calm. I'm trying to help you. If it won't go up it will have to come down.'

The irrefutable scientific logic of this remark seemed to soothe the Sir Irwin who sat motionless and resigned like a falcon, hooded, upon its block.

Graham exerted all the pressure he dared without actually driving the victim's neck down between his shoulders, with the result that the wrecked bowler suddenly flew downwards, throwing Graham flat on his face in the heather.

'Thank God, I can see. I can see.'

'Of course you can damn well see . . . Christ . . . It's Sir Irwin Broadchalke.'

'MacCallister . . . Thank heavens it's you and not that army lunatic.'

'What army lunatic, Sir Irwin? There seem to be quite a few of them about.'

'Do there? Do there, my boy? Well the sooner we get somewhere safe the better.'

Limping badly, Dr Braithwaite appeared from the gulley into which he had fallen when Pomona tripped him.

'They've all gone bonkers,' he announced. 'You all right, Sir Irwin? . . . Hullo, who the hell are *you*?'

'Graham MacCallister. NERTS deer project. I'm studying droppings.'

'Fascinating,' said Braithwaite. 'We must have a long talk about it some time. For the moment, all I want to do is to get off this bloody battlefield.'

'You'd better all come to NERTS HQ'

'Sounds very appropriate.'

'Shouldn't we try to get this other chap on his feet?'

'Poor old Sniffy. He seems to have copped a packet. Is that army captain completely round the twist?'

'Pomona? No. He's normally pretty level-headed.'

'Bullet-headed is more like it.'

Colonel Snettisham was beginning to stir. Together they

hauled him to his feet. Supporting him with arms linked around his shoulders, Graham and Dr Braithwaite started back for the cottages. Sir Irwin brought up the rear, from time to time glancing fearfully back.

Perhaps because of his nearness to Mother Earth and all her creatures, MacGregor found no difficulty in behaving like either a stag or a blackcock, or, if necessary, both. After pursuing the terrified Roxborough up the village street on his scrambler, he had decided to go in search of Flora Flodden, or failing her, any other greyhen that offered. So he had fetched his bagpipes from the cottage, mounted his motor-bike again and headed out to the grassy meadow where the Scottish contingent was encamped.

The Scotsmen plus Jerry Mathews were at it when he arrived. Yet nothing very positive seemed to come from any of it. Plainly the dance, or was it lek? had not yet worked itself up to the required pitch. MacGregor decided to warm things up. He rode straight in amongst the dancers at full bore. Then, holding the throttle open with one hand, and fingering his pipes with the other, he conjured up a wild and warlike skirl that was two thirds bagpipes and one third exhaust note.

The results were startling. The tempo of the dancing among the males increased to a frenzy. Women started to appear from among the tents. Occupied as he was by the dual demands of riding and playing, MacGregor nevertheless noted that Flora Flodden was nowhere to be seen. Perhaps she had joined up with the red deer group. He had a mind's-eye picture of the brutish Hammond Hulke galloping down on her. Aye! He'd have to put paid to that. Ever since things had started happening to them all, he'd felt himself to be more a stag than a blackcock. This was the last time he'd come lekking. A lek, he felt, was not so manly as a good old-fashioncd rut. Still, now he'd stirred them all up, he might as well take advantage of the situation.

The circle in which he was riding had gradually widened out until he had reached the boundary where the meadow joined a neighbouring spinney. Jeannie McCall had cannily observed this and had cut across so that she met

MacGregor and the snarling Greaves just when they were running out of ground. Jeannie stood triumphantly and beckoningly in their path. With a wild whoop, MacGregor flung his bagpipes into a gorse bush, opened the throttle wide and leapt vertically out of the saddle, allowing the scrambler to career forward on its own until it toppled into some scrub willow. Jeannie neatly side-stepped the machine and, seizing MacGregor as he landed, led him off into the nearby thicket. As she pulled him through the undergrowth a phrase from Dr Jerry Mathews' lecture came back to her.

'Blackcock and greyhens seldom mate actually on the lekking ground.'

When Captain Pomona reached his office he was both relieved and surprised to discover Corporal Gunnersbury on duty. His little command had deteriorated so rapidly that he was quite prepared to find his orders completely ignored and the radio in the orderly room unmanned.

Gunnersbury rose to his feet in some semblance of a military manner and saluted with his one good hand.

Pomona returned the salute. The act of raising his arm flung a swathe of water across the room.

'Hulke push you into the burn?' Corporal Gunnersbury asked conversationally.

'Yes. How did you know?'

'He did it to Dr Mathews yesterday.'

'Good heavens. Does he make a habit of it?'

'Seems to be his favourite dodge, sir. He's a terror. Notice all that muscle he's putting on round the shoulders lately?'

'He's always been pretty heavily built.'

'Nothing to what he is now. He's said to be doing a lot of peeing, too. As a matter of fact we all are. Mason and I, too, even though we've got busted antlers, sorry limbs. Urinating like it was going out of fashion. Don't know where it all comes from. Seems we all sort of save it up. A squirt here, a slash there. Noticed anything unusual yourself, sir?'

'Now you come to mention it, Gunnersbury, my bladder does seem, well, a bit weak. I had to stop two or three times on the way back here,' added Pomona, wondering just what the devil he was doing discussing his urinary problems with Corporal Gunnersbury. 'What's it all about?' he heard himself asking.

'According to that Dr Roxborough, it's all to do with marking out one's territory.'

Corporal Gunnersbury viewed with concern the puddle in which Captain Pomona was now standing.

'You haven't? . . . There's no need to mark out your territory in the office, sir. We know you're in charge here. I mean the orderly room has to be sort of neutral ground, though I don't suppose that bastard Hulke would recognise the fact.'

'Pull yourself together, Corporal,' Pomona said trying hard to do exactly that himself. 'Can't you see I'm dripping wet. It's all running down my leg.'

The Corporal felt it wasn't his place to comment on this. 'Very good, sir. If you'd just like to change into some dry clothes I'll make you a mug of char. When in doubt, brew up. That's my motto. Mustn't forget we're in the good old British Army.'

Captain Pomona found it increasingly hard to keep this fact in mind.

Janet Morgan saw the battered expeditionary force approaching up the village street and immediately put on the kettle.

'What happened, Graham. Did it crash?'

'The chopper? No. Pomona and Hulke have gone berserk.'

Graham made the introductions.

'You're far too beautiful to be a scientist, my dear,' Dr Braithwaite said.

'Nevertheless she is one and she happens to work for me.' Sir Irwin had recovered slightly. 'So does this young man. And Dr Hammond Hulke, though I'm beginning to think I picked the wrong man there. From what little you've told me, MacCallister, he appears to be raving mad. Homicidal almost. What about Roxborough by the way?'

'You might say that he's moderately raving.'

'You two seem fairly normal. You *are* by the way, I suppose?'

'Ye . . . es.'

'You appear hesitant, MacCallister.'

'He's as normal as I am, Sir Irwin,' Janet said.

Graham looked at her closely. Was even the cool Janet quite as normal as she'd been before that moonlight night on Ben Dhui?

'Oh yes,' Graham said. 'Then what about the singing in the ears?'

Raymond Braithwaite asked: 'Singing in the ears? Perhaps you'd better tell me about it. When did you first notice it?'

'After we'd been up the mountain together on the night of the rutting moon.'

'Ah,' said Sir Irwin. 'Possibly the altitude . . .'

'Ben Dhui's only just 3000 feet,' Graham told him.

Dr Braithwaite said knowingly: 'Well, of course, a moonlight night on the mountain together might account for anything.'

Sir Irwin's natural gift for leadership returned with every sip of Janet's tea.

'I suggest that we should try not to be frivolous.'

Somewhere, far away outside, a bugle blew a wild cracked note, a loud-hailer answered and a motor-bike engine roared defiance.

Forgetting his plea for solemnity, Sir Irwin demanded: 'Will someone tell me just what the hell is going on around here?'

'They're roaring, rather belling, at each other. Just like rutting stags. There's a blackcock lek, too.'

'Good God,' Sir Irwin drunk the rest of his tea at a swallow. 'It's impossible, unthinkable.'

'Chronic hormonal imbalance.' Dr Braithwaite sounded delirious with joy. 'It's just possible. Aided by the powerful suggestion of everything taking place around them in nature.'

'And the NERTS study programme.' Sir Irwin meant to see that his department got all possible credit.

'Dr Roxborough and Jerry Mathews gave the Tracking

Unit talks on rutting and lekking,' Graham told them.

'Did they, by God? And who authorised *that*?' Sir Irwin demanded.

'No matter who authorised it,' the doctor said, 'auto-suggestion or even mass hypnotism couldn't alone account for what seems to be taking place here.'

'Those dancers we flew over were behaving just like lekking blackcock,' Sir Irwin agreed. 'And Pomona was definitely a sneaky rutter, creeping in on the hinds when the master stag was occupied.'

'What did he take *us* for?' the doctor asked.

'Other sneaky rutters?'

'In bowler hats?'

'If you're right about severe hormonal disturbance, doctor, headgear would make very little difference to the aggressor's mentality. It might even aggravate it. After all, what does a rutting stag often do?'

'You tell me, Sir Irwin.'

'It decorates its antlers with grass and peat mire, to make itself look more formidable.'

'I don't think Lock's of St James's Street would consider that much of an advertisement.'

'Maybe not, but there's little doubt my antlers, I mean bowler, saved me from a severe case of concussion. If poor old Snettisham's hat had stayed on when his head hit the rock, he'd probably be okay, too.'

They looked sympathetically at the inert figure of the Colonel who had been wrapped by Janet in a blanket. His eyelids were just beginning to flutter.

'Tell me, dear,' Dr Braithwaite was all Harley Street manner, 'have you or your friend exhibited any, forgive me, rutting – indelicate sort of word that – anyway, abnormal rutting symptoms?'

'Nothing that I'm aware of, Doctor.' Janet made an effort to become scientifically detached. 'I agree that I did have this singing in the ears for two days after the full moon.'

Braithwaite considered his notes. 'That would be the night of October tenth. The night you were up the mountain?'

'Yes, Doctor.'

'And it wore off about twenty-four hours ago?'

'Correct.'

'Any further symptoms?'

Graham blurted out: 'She's become a lot more friendly recently.'

Raymond Braithwaite raised his eyebrows comically. It was a gesture he often used in his consulting room to convey that, no matter how lurid the information disclosed by a patient, he was, apart from being one of the most highly qualified, not to say paid, of his profession, a man of the world.

'That may or may not be related to the circumstances we have been sent to investigate.'

'Oh,' said Graham. 'Then it isn't just a routine inspection like the signal said?'

'I hardly think we should divulge . . .' began Sir Irwin.

'Surely we have to take this apparently normal, hopefully unaffected, and certainly intelligent and attractive young couple into our confidence. They may be able to help us, to borrow a phrase from the police, in our enquiries.'

'How do we know they're quite normal?' Sir Irwin demanded.

'Yes, how do you know? Perhaps I should tell you about the appalling irritation at the front of my skull,' Graham blurted out. 'For about forty-eight hours it nearly drove me mad. Mind you, I didn't have it half so badly as some of the army chaps.' He pointed towards the front of his luxuriant red hair. 'Here and here.'

Sir Irwin spread his hands with the gesture of a QC who feels his case is proved without need for another word. Nevertheless he did speak one more word: '*Normal?*'

'What's a scalp itch? We all have them from time to time,' argued the doctor. 'Probably mosquitoes or clegs or whatever foul biting insects they have in this wilderness area.'

'I suppose it hadn't occurred to you,' Sir Irwin said, 'that the points indicated by MacCallister are precisely where stags grow their new antlers each year.'

'No,' said Braithwaite, impressed despite himself, 'it hadn't.'

'And then,' added Graham, 'there are my faecal pellets.'

'Beg pardon.' Raymond Braithwaite was used to hearing most things medical, but this shook even him a little.

'They're radioactive.'

'Jesus' said the doctor.

'Beyond the normal level one would expect.'

'Are you in the habit of checking regularly?'

'I'm doing a faeces study,' said Graham. 'It's a somewhat limited field but I hope to branch out later.'

'You mean your . . . er stools are radioactive.'

'Not *mine*. The red deer droppings. I've done several tests. They're far more radioactive suddenly than one has any right to expect.'

At the second use of the word 'radioactive' Colonel Sniffy Snettisham surfaced and sat bolt upright.

'We must take proper readings,' he announced. 'At once. All over the island.'

He slumped into a semi-coma again.

Late October

The helicopter pilot was relaxing over his second malt in the oilmen's bar. He had flown an ITN news crew out to a new offshore rig where there was said to be an imminent risk of a major leak. The visit had not been a success. They had been greeted as they circled the rig's heli-pad with a flak barrage of well-directed steam hoses. When they did manage to land they had been welcomed by the rig boss with a blow-out of language which even Red Adair might have found difficult to seal. Finally, there was no danger of a leak and had been no danger of a leak. It appeared that the whole thing had been a malicious canard put about by one of the nuttier conservation groups concerned for the welfare of a nearby puffin colony. The ITN crew had shot a few feet for stock of the firehose welcome, decided that the interview with the rig boss was definitely not for family viewing and had returned to base on the mainland.

'I'm not going back without a story,' Nigel Newman, the ITN interviewer said for about the tenth time. He had recently transferred from the BBC where he had made a name as a young lion who was never happier than when ducking about amid shot and shell with dusky rioters tripping over his microphone cable.

'We could always,' said his cameraman, 'knock off a piece about how the locals are reacting to the oil boom.'

'Oh, do me a favour, Ed.'

'Or interview the madame of the oilmen's brothel. There's no crumpet out on the rigs. Or booze either.'

This was the soundman's suggestion. A short, fat lecherous man, he was known as Gus the Grope.

'True or false?' Newman asked the chopper pilot.

'I've never bothered to find out. There's plenty of the real thing around here just spoiling for want of proper care and attention. All these canteen waitresses and such.'

They ordered another round.

'Tell you what, Nige,' (they were on abbreviated Christian name terms by this time). 'Tell you what, old son. Two days ago I had a very strange bunch of weirdos to take out to Horn.'

'To *where*?'

'Horn. It's a remote island about seventy-five miles off. Got a radar tracking station and some kind of scientific outfit on it. Well, these three guys wore bowler hats and carried rolled umbrellas . . .'

'You're making it up,' said Ed, the cameraman.

'Hell of a name for an island,' said Gus the Grope. 'You made that up, too. Horn! It's too bloody good to be true.'

'Well, it *is* true,' said the pilot. 'And if you don't believe the bit about the bowler hats, you certainly won't believe what happened when I finally landed these clubland commandos.'

'A good phrase,' Nigel said. 'I could use that. What did happen?'

The pilot told them in lurid detail.

'Are they all crackers?' Nigel demanded.

'Search me. It's all very hush-hush. The geezer in charge told me that.'

'Who was he?'

'Toffee-nosed old bastard called Sir Irwin Broadchalke.'

'He's the head NERT,' Nigel said.

'I shouldn't be at all surprised.'

'Who were the other two?'

'Hold on a sec. I've still got my passenger list somewhere. Yes, Dr Raymond Braithwaite and Colonel Snettisham, MOD.

'I know Snettisham,' Nigel said excitedly. 'I interviewed him on a NATO exercise in Germany. He's a nuclear expert, specialises in dealing with the after-effects of atomic attack.'

Gus the Grope was losing interest. As a soundman he liked a few good challenging bangs and high-pitched whines from jet engines. 'Talking of NATO, isn't there some sort of naval exercise taking place off Scotland? Why don't we cover that?'

'Because, you fat, ignorant sound recordist, ITN already

has a crew aboard our only warship and more than three passengers tend to make her capsize . . . No, this Horn thing intrigues me. Broadchalke's a career scientist, but he's also and environmentalist. A funny combination, he and Snettisham. Then this doctor chap.'

'Probably a shrink,' suggested Ed, the cameraman. 'Sounds as though they all need a shrink.'

'Listen,' Nigel had made a decision. 'I think it's worth a look. When can you nip us over to Horn? It'll only take an hour.'

'Sorry, Nige. No can do. I'm under strict orders not to go back until called up on the radio. More than my job's worth.'

'Okay, then someone else will have to take us.'

'No go. The other two choppers are fully chartered by the oil companies.'

'How else can we get there?'

'No way. No, wait a minute. There's a clapped-out trawler called the *Haddie* that delivers supplies to Horn once a fortnight. She must be due to leave any day now.'

'Who's her skipper? Where do I find him?'

'He's a tall, thin, hard-drinking, barely intelligible, utterly unlovable local character called MacTavert. You'll find him in the "Twa Boobies". He'll be well into the malt by now. After nine p.m. he usually only speaks in the Gaelic.'

'What's "Twa Boobies" mean?' Gus the Grope asked hopefully.

'Two gannets, I think.'

'Oh!' Gus sounded crushed. 'I thought perhaps it meant tits. What a barbaric lot they are up here. No culture.'

For the ladies of Myfanwy Preece's little band – she now referred to her detachment as a herd – every day was a strange one and every succeeding day stranger than its predecessor.

Take the day before yesterday for example, the day on which the helicopter had so mysteriously dropped its trio of bowler-hatted invaders, the day on which Pomona had got his come-uppance from Hulke.

After demonstrating with a series of hoarse bellows that

he was the undisputed master of the situation, Hulke had ordered the women out of their tents and then driven them up the hill towards a grassy corrie some two hundred feet above their camp. The scampering, half-alarming, half-exciting nature of the climb had left the girls breathless. Dr Whymper, especially, had found it heavy going. Every time she lagged behind, or even paused to catch her breath, there had been Hulke circling warily below her, red of face and bloodshot of eye, forcing her to keep up with the rest of the women. It was quite terrifying really and yet she sensed Hulke had no ruttish designs on her. Instinctively, Regina Whymper knew that her time had come and passed. Her finest hour had been with Bertram in the officers' quarters. She was no longer interested in him or anyone else. It was just as if she had enjoyed a brief season, a period of *oestrus*, and that her state of sexual receptiveness, nay eagerness, had passed like an autumn storm. Now she intuitively knew that a long winter of lovelessness lay ahead. Nevertheless, she shied in alarm each time that Hulke roared. Each woman was dimly aware that he or she was conforming to some ritualised behaviour pattern that was not theirs to question.

At least one part, the trained part, of the MO's mind remained functioning comparatively normally. Her job, even in the present topsy-turvy circumstances, was to look after her girls' health. Earlier that morning, back in camp, she had held her weekly medical parade. At this it was her custom to issue any medical stores needed to keep the ladies of the Radar Tracking Unit in tip-top operational condition. This was the moment at which Dr Whymper handed out replenishment supplies of the Pill. Nobody, after all, wanted, as Dr Whymper was apt to say with military whimsicality, any new recruits added to the ration strength.

She invariably found her girls only too eager to accept a free issue of Pills, Contraceptive. That morning she was amazed to discover that every single girl – the pattern had been repeated among the Scottish contingent when she had later visited Blackcock camp – had vehemently turned down her free offer.

Private Gwladys Stopham was first to refuse.

'No thank you, doctor.'

The MO essayed a little joke: 'Don't you want to . . . er . . . stop 'em?'

'Nature has to take its course, doctor. As a matter of fact, I stopped taking the Pill nearly a week ago.'

'I see. You realise what you may be doing . . . I mean . . . You haven't exactly concealed your private life since we moved under canvas.'

'None of us has, doctor.'

'Quite,' said the MO quickly. 'Well . . . er, good luck, Private Stopham. I think perhaps I had better have a word with your section officer.'

When all the ladies had repeated Gwladys Stopham's refusal, Dr Whymper called Myfanwy Preece aside.

'Are they all going crazy?'

'Don't you mean, aren't *we* all going crazy? I suppose you've been taking yours?'

'Well, no, actually.'

'There you are then.'

'But in my case there's no need.'

Myfanwy's rolled her eyes. 'That's not the way I heard it, or saw it, for that matter.'

'Does everyone want to get pregnant?'

'Seems like it. After all, that's nature's way.'

After their initial reverses, the bowler-hatted commando force had regrouped. They had consolidated with local elements in the shape of Janet Morgan and Graham MacCallister and established a bridgehead with its command post at the NERTS cottage formerly occupied by Doctors Hulke and Roxborough. They had moved into action with a speed and efficiency of which the Prime Minister would have been proud.

For the two days since they landed, Graham MacCallister, under the semi-conscious and not always lucid direction of Sniffy Snettisham, had been tramping the island taking Geiger counter readings from the tip of the Tine of Ben Dhui down to the ruggedest rocks at sea level.

The Colonel, still recovering from severe concussion,

remained propped up in an armchair before the fire at NERTS HQ co-ordinating the radioactive sampling and assessing the results. Occasionally his concussion caused him to wander. However, on the morning of the third day, he felt both sufficiently confident of his findings and recovered from his head injuries to give a speculative appreciation of the situation. All he waited for now was for Graham to return with the final set of readings from the island's west coast.

Sir Irwin had played a commendably front-line part in the investigation. In his youth he had stalked red deer with a Scottish uncle in Sutherland. It was this early sporting interest that had, in fact, turned his steps towards zoology. His Ph.D. thesis had been on the role of trace elements in antler growth. Now, the prospect of being able to crawl about in the heather again observing with a deer-stalker's glass appealed to him greatly. The difference was that this time he wasn't going to observe deer so much as people behaving like deer and, if young MacCallister could be believed, not only deer but blackcock also. So for two days now, Sir Irwin, supported by Janet Morgan, had been out every hour that daylight gave watching the behaviour of the females at Hind and Blackcock camps and from time to time that of Hulke, Roxborough, Markham, MacGregor and other itinerant and plainly less dominant males. He, too had reached some shattering, if tentative conclusions.

Dr Raymond Braithwaite's role had been, perhaps, the hardest of all because it required the most tact. His first task had been to make some rather personal tests and obtain samples from a cross-section of those who might have been affected by Ted Illingworth's radioactive leak. Persuasive as he was with patients, Braithwaite did not fancy the idea of breezing into Blackcock or Hind camps and simply asking the inmates to provide him with a specimen or two.

Raymond Braithwaite found his first two guinea-pigs readily enough.

Both Janet and Graham were not only keen to show their scientific objectivity, they were desperately intent to prove that they were completely normal. Throughout a lengthy examination, both physiological and pyschological, Dr Braithwaite had maintained that Olympian calm that his Harley Street clientele found so initially soothing and so ultimately costly. Graham MacCallister was not soothed.

'Am I or am I not one hundred per cent normal?'

'Well, in the end, possibly you are the best judge of that.'

'Oh, don't do the bedside bit, doctor.'

'Call me Raymond, please.'

'Okay, Raymond. What's the score then? Am I or am I not radioactive?'

'As a scientist, Graham, you must know that one just can't rush to conclusions. The tests have got to be analysed and evaluated.'

'Oh hell, Raymond. Sometimes I feel I'd like to butt you in the pit of the stomach like old Pomona did.'

'Do you now? *Do* you?'

'You know I only said that as a joke.'

'Of course.' Raymond Braithwaite was at his smoothest. 'I must be off to the Army. Sir Irwin tells me that Captain Pomona spends most of his time at his headquarters.'

'Mind he doesn't charge you on sight.'

'Somehow, I don't think he'll do that. Sir Irwin's field notes suggest that he's passing out of what we might call his intensive rutting state rather earlier than the other males. Besides, I expect his training as a regular officer to persuade him to play ball with me.'

With memories of his recent physical examination still fresh, Graham said: 'I should have thought you could have chosen a more Harley Street phrase.'

'Nice to see you're not losing your sense of humour, Graham. Ah well, I must be off. Sir Irwin wants a reassuring signal sent to the Prime Minister.'

'How about: "Wish you were here. Great place for a stag party?"'

'Very good, Graham, but somehow I don't think the Prime Minister would appreciate it.'

'Anything from Horn yet?' the Prime Minister asked his PPS.

'Signal just come in, sir.'

'Good, what does it say?'

'It's to Officer in Command Scottish Tracking Stations from Captain Pomona, Officer in Command, Horn, sir. It reads: "Your routine inspection party landed in middle of energetic and realistic training exercise. Casualties fortunately light confined mainly to bowler hats and one case possible concussion. Suggest bowlers and umbrellas unsuitable for local conditions. Will endeavour issue more practical clothing from stores. O/C Horn."'

The Prime Minister paled. 'God, they've beaten up poor old Broadchalke.'

'Or Snettisham,'

'Far too tough.'

'Or Braithwaite.'

'Far too smart.'

'Don't forget Gilbey at Dundoom, sir.'

'I wish I could.'

'I mean how violent he got.'

'How is Gilbey, by the way?'

'The news seems to be good, sir. The Ministry of Energy reports he's calming down. They've got him out of a strait-jacket now.'

'That's nice, then.'

'The Ministry doctor reports his voice appears to be breaking.'

'Bit late for that, isn't it?'

'*Upwards*, sir. Into the treble range.'

'Ted Illingworth's got a lot to answer for. See that Gilbey's kept in complete isolation. We don't want him assaulting choir boys next.'

'No danger of that, sir. In the last twenty-four hours he seems to have lost interest in sex entirely. Definitely eunuchoid symptoms, the report says.'

'Whatever Illingworth unleashed on the community, the stuff seems to act very fast,' thc Primc Minister said moodily. 'Keep me posted.'

The SS *Haddie* stuck her blunt, rusting bows into a mountainously broken sea and dug them in like a pig rooting for turnips. She kept her head down as if it was anchored there and allowed her screw to race until it seemed the last corroded rivet must pop out of her hull with the vibration. She came up at last just in time to catch a green, quartering sea that slewed her sideways with a horrible lurch. She appeared actually to be enjoying the whole sickening performance. She repeated it with variations. When she finally rose up again and toppled over the crest of the swell she shook her ancient hull like a labrador freeing its coat of water. Wedged against the binnacle, Nigel Newman of ITN waited for the wheelhouse to be swept clean from the deck with each sea that came creaming over the bulwarks. He would have been sick for the sixth time if the fifth time hadn't already exhausted his potential.

'I'll no upset your stomach if I light my pipe?'

The storm had made the taciturn Captain MacTavert unusually talkative.

Nigel gagged at the suggestion. The slight twitch of his features was evidently taken by MacTavert as an encouragement to smoke. Balancing himself against the side of the dodger, he extracted from the side of one seaboot a black stick of plug which could easily have been dynamite, and possibly was. He began to teazle it with a sheath-knife. The holding, the scraping, the catching of the plug shavings were all expertly performed with the right hand while the left held the bucking wheel whose wild gyrations appeared to be totally unconnected with any steering influence on the part of the rudder.

Nigel waited in desperation for the shavings of plug to be tamped into the pipe. The cloud of smoke mercifully streamed aft on the gale, though eddies occasionally wafted back. Nigel now thought he knew what an Arbroath Smokie went through in the curing process.

'How long's the trip going to take?' he managed to gasp at last.

'In this wee bit of a blow? Mebbe six hours, mebbe twelve. It dusna' matter. It's grand to get a breath of sea air in your lungs, laddie.'

Captain MacTavert exhaled a dense cloud of plug fumes whose blue-grey interior was lit by sparks of burning tobacco that shot upwards inside it like lumps of molten magma in a volcanic explosion.

'Ye'll take a dram, Mr Newman?'

Nigel nodded agreement. He couldn't trust himself to speak while the after-effects of the recent eruption lingered in his lungs.

Clamping the lower spokes of the wheel with his long, thin, sea-booted legs, MacTavert reached for a stone jug that was held securely against the worst roll that *Haddie* could contrive in a specially recessed shelf. He slurped himself a quarter of a pint of his home-distilled malt into a similarly held enamel mug, swallowed half of it at a gulp and handed the rest to Nigel. Nigel waited for the ship to hurl the mug towards his face and somehow managed to project an amber gush of liquid into his mouth. To his amazement it did not immediately melt his stomach lining. At once he felt a benign glow as though life itself was being recreated in his vitals. It didn't taste bad either. The general effect was as if he had inhaled the gentle smoke of a peat fire while being given a strangely stimulating, though not unpleasant shock of, say, around 1000 volts.

MacTavert saw that he had saved a life and murmured '*Usquebaugh*,' the Gaelic word for the true malt whisky, which means 'the water of life'.

'Have the other half, laddie.'

MacTavert poured another generous slug, drank three quarters of it himself and handed the remainder to Nigel.

While all this had been going on, the *Haddie* had been pleasing herself even more than usual. She was now heading south-east, instead of north-west.

'Ah, ye auld bitch,' her Captain scolded and spun the wheel so many times it seemed it must fall off.

'She's no listening. I'll teach the old cow.' MacTavert opened the throttle of her puffing diesel to full speed. Surprisingly, the ancient trawler leapt ahead and did so with such enthusiasm that she seemed determined to turn herself into a submarine. When she surfaced at last, she was almost on the right heading again.

'Look out!' Nigel shouted.

A mile ahead and bearing down fast was the long grey

shape of a warship flying the white ensign. The knife-edge bows slicing that horrible sea seemed to be aimed directly at the SS *Haddie*.

'He's going to run us down.'

'He's got to give way to sail.'

'You're not under sail.'

'Compared to yon floating gin palace, we are.'

'Perhaps he hasn't seen us.'

'Aye, he got us on the radar, never fear. He's got to make way and he knows it.'

It occurred to Nigel that the warship which he now recognised as a missile destroyer was finding it impossible to guess just which way the *Haddie* was heading.

'Perhaps he thinks we're a spy trawler.'

'He knows us right enough. I'll give him a blast on the hooter.'

MacTavert did so more for personal satisfaction than anything else since the sound must have been lost on the gale.

At what appeared to be the last moment bar one, the destroyer heeled over to starboard, executed a neat turn and came racing up on the weather side to offer the shelter of her port quarter.

'Told you I'd make him obey the law of the sea.'

From the wing of the warship's bridge an officer with a loud-hailer called: 'Are you under control?'

'Is that all you've got to do with taxpayer's money, sailor boy?' MacTavert bellowed back through a megaphone.

The figure on the bridge tried again.

'Are you fishing?'

'Aw awa' and fush yerself,' or anyway that's what it sounded like.

The Officer of the Watch waved cheerily. 'Good luck, thought you might be a Russki.'

'Run away and play boats, sonny,' MacTavert advised and, with a sudden creaming of its wake, the destroyer did so.

Sir Irwin Broadchalke addressed his team of experts.

'Gentlemen and Dr Morgan,' he said. 'It is four days

since our mission landed, four busy, astonishing and in some ways very disturbing days. The Prime Minister will be anxiously awaiting an interim report on our activities here. I believe that we are all of the opinion that we are, in our several fields, in a position to give such a report.'

Sir Irwin swept the table with his penetrating look famous in scientific committees throughout the land.

'I don't think I need point out to Mr MacCallister and Dr Morgan that we are all of us bound by the Official Secrets Acts. Colonel Snettisham, I will call on you first. Do remain seated, please. I know that that blow on the head is still troubling you.'

Sniffy Snettisham made an gallant effort to stand but felt himself swaying and sat down quickly. 'Prime Minister's no fool,' he said. 'Should have kept my bowler on. Thought at the time that bowlers were a bit inappropriate, but the Prime Minister knew . . .' The Colonel appeared to be wandering. He clasped his head.

'Take your time, Colonel. Perhaps we could start with the map.'

'Ah, yes. The map.' The Colonel focused his concussed pupils with considerable effort on the large map of Horn spread on the table.

'MacCallister here, under my direction, has been taking detailed Geiger counter readings of the areas most affected by radioactivity.' The Colonel indicated the map.

'The red-shaded portions are the ones most heavily exposed. You will notice that they include all the low-lying ground. Contamination remains fairly constant until we reach the 1500 foot contour line, indicated by pink colouring. From there on upwards, until we get to 3000 feet on the Tine of Ben Dhui, the effect of the gas cloud becomes less and less marked. Between 2000 and 3000 feet the radioactivity decreases fast.'

'As borne out by my faecal pellets,' Graham said excitedly.

'Precisely.'

Janet said: 'That's where Graham and I were that night – between 2500 and 3000 feet. That's why it missed us.'

'I think,' said Sir Irwin, 'we may be getting ahead of the

game. If we could just confine ourselves to the Colonel's report.'

The Colonel was having difficulty concentrating again. 'Done my bit, really,' he said, passing his hand across his eyes. 'Not much more to add. Maybe Sir Irwin would like to carry on from here . . .'

'I rather think we'd better hear from Dr Braithwaite next.'

Raymond Braithwaite stood up. 'My impressions are exactly that . . . just impressions. As you will appreciate, I have been unable to obtain medical co-operation from the occupants of either Blackcock or Hind camps. Not even Captain Pomona, who has tried his best to help, has been able to penetrate what I feel I must call the herds. However, he has agreed to tests being carried out on himself and the two NCOs, Gunnersbury and Mason, who at present comprise his headquarters staff. I have also examined their injuries and learnt how they were caused. You gentlemen, and Dr Morgan, have been kind enough to agree to examination also.'

Sir Irwin said: 'Don't tell us we're affected. I suppose it could happen. Residual radiation, after-effects and so on.'

'I can reassure you,' said Braithwaite. 'None of we three shows any signs of the changes that have undoubtedly occurred in the other inhabitants of Horn . . . so far.'

'What about Janet and I?'

'High as you were that night on the mountain the radiation obviously didn't miss you entirely. You, Graham, have had some secondary symptoms. Singing in the ears, for instance. And the dual irritation of the scalp. Janet, too. Her ears sang for a bit.'

'At least she hasn't shown any urge to go off and join the rest of the girls like Flora or Joanna.'

'I agree. But that's not to say that she won't exhibit further symptoms. You, too, Graham for that matter.'

Janet laughed nervously. 'I may not be in a state of *oestrus* yet. Is that what you mean?'

'Okay. If you want to put it like that. It may not happen. From the tests I've made, I'd say it's pretty unlikely.'

'But you'd like to keep Graham and me under observation.'

'I think that's a fair summary of the situation.'

'Perhaps,' Sir Irwin suggested, 'we could return to the wider picture.'

'Very well then. There is no doubt that the radioactivity on Horn has, as we suspected, produced a violent, rapid and hitherto unknown hormonal imbalance.'

'Irreversible?' asked Sir Irwin.

'I'm afraid it's far too early to say. What it appears to have done is to have erased all the normal sex-drives. Such feelings have been replaced, almost overnight, by a period of intense sexual activity as observed among certain species of mammals and birds.'

'In this instance,' Sir Irwin broken in, 'blackcock and red deer.'

'Thank you, Sir Irwin,' said Braithwaite. 'If we may, we'll come to the nature notes in a moment. But, since you raise the point, one is bound to ask why the victims of this radioactive accident should have elected to adopt the sexual behaviour of those two species? The questions of course, cannot be answered without considerable physiological and psychological research. The actual physical effects of the radiation are real beyond any question. Among the stags, and I feel I must call them that, consider only the symbolic itching of the forehead where the antlers should grow, the deepening of the voice . . .'

Graham coughed nervously as if trying out his vocal chords.

'The roaring or, as I believe it's called, belling. The outright aggression when faced with another male. A similar behaviour pattern is seen among what I will call the cocks on the blackcock lek. The adoption of the kilt as a display dress. Male sparring and dancing.

'As for the females, whom we should think of as hens or hinds, there seems little doubt, as Janet mentioned just now, that they are entering brief periods or seasons when they are ready and eager to be mated. This is particularly noticeable, as Sir Irwin will no doubt tell you, among the girls of Hind camp. It would appear to me, admittedly without the benefit of physical examination of the ladies, impossible because of the present aggressive attention of the resident stags . . .

'It would seem to me that the ladies are entering a brief period of *oestrus* very similar to that of a red deer hind. This lasts three or four days at the most. During that period they are, apparently, available to the dominant male. Thereafter, they show no interest in any other stag, and certainly not in the stag with whom, before the radioactive leak, they were enjoying a sexual relationship. Now the interesting point is this. Why stags and blackcock? Why hinds and greyhens? If the hormonal balance of both sexes was to be seriously disturbed, then might not the victims of this radioactivity have started behaving like any other member of the animal kingdom that crams its sex life into a short period of frenzied activity? Why aren't the men and women of Captain Pomona's command, and Dr Roxborough's NERTS, too, acting like, say, baboons or gorillas?'

'Seems to me they are,' murmured Snettisham, 'that chap who attacked me was distinctly baboon-like.'

Raymond Braithwaite ignored the interruption. 'I submit as a tentative hypothesis . . .'

'Hypotheses must, by definition, be tentative,' said Sir Irwin. He was getting tired of Raymond Braithwaite holding the floor.

'Be that as it may,' went on the doctor. 'It does not seem beyond the bounds of possibility that mass hypnotism of some kind may have a bearing on the fact that the victims have chosen to be deer or blackcock. The very atmosphere of Horn. The presence of the deer and blackcock all around them. The activities of Sir Irwin's NERTS, and, not least, the course of lectures given to the troops. All these may have influenced these, shall I call them, human deer and grouse once the violent hormonal changes had been initiated in their systems. I leave you with that suggestion.'

Sir Irwin smoothed back his iron grey hair and stood up.

'Thank you, Doctor. I'm sure we all enjoyed your

summary, particularly the buoyancy with which your fancy latterly took flight on somewhat unscientific wings, if I may put it that way. My own notes will be brief and concerned only with actual observations made in the field.

'First for the blackcock. In the last twenty-four hours there has been a marked decrease in lekking activity. I believe that the mating season among the blackcock, who, I deduce from their dress, consist mainly of the Scots element in the Tracking Unit, is nearly over. I think we can assume,' Sir Irwin coughed slightly to emphasise his ornithological funny, 'that most of the greyhens will shortly be carrying fertile eggs. Since the shepherd MacGregor appears to have been a much sought after . . . er cock . . . it seems safe to suppose that the representatives of the clan MacGregor will enjoy a marked increase on the Island of Horn at the end of the assorted greyhens', er, incubation period.'

'Poor Joanna,' Janet sighed.

'You never know,' Graham reassured her, 'Jerry may have well, you know, got at her first.'

'"Trodden her" is the phrase,' put in Sir Irwin.

'Sounds very ungallant,' Braithwaite murmured.

'I doubt if he made it,' said Janet. 'He was obviously subdominant. That eclipse plumage of his . . .'

'I'll carry on, if I may, Dr Morgan.' Sir Irwin was icily polite.

'MacGregor presents a most unusual case. He appears to be sexually dimorphic or, more accurately, dispecific. As someone has, I believe, already observed: he doesn't appear to know whether he's a blackcock or a stag. Suffice it to say that he has been both treading hens and covering hinds. A man of most unusual energy. Moreover unlike the rest of the radioactively affected males on this island, though he shares his services generously, he appears to be partial to one female in particular. I have observed three separate couplings, two on the lek and one in the shepherd's bothy known, I believe, as the shearing shed. The lady concerned is by no means the youngest or most nubile of the available breeding stock. However, this is entirely in keeping with the behaviour patterns of both grouse and red deer. To him she is obviously either a mature hen or perhaps a hind of at least eight years, whichever way MacGregor is currently looking at things.'

'Flora Flodden!' said Janet.

'He finally made it, and in the shearing shed, too,' Graham broke in. 'He said he would that night on the Tine when we heard the master stag belling. The Gaelic magic came true for MacGregor.' Graham looked longingly at Janet.

'I don't know what you're talking about MacCallister, but I'm afraid magic, Gaelic or otherwise, doesn't account for MacGregor's superhuman stamina. Let us now pass on to the other stags.' Sir Irwin consulted his field notes. 'First we have the two sub-adults, the junior NCOs Gunnersbury and Mason. Both were injured in early rutting fights with a mature and well-antlered stag who started with the obvious dominance given him by his rank. I refer, of course, to CSM Markham. The decisive encounter between these three took place – and I have both Gunnersbury's and Mason's account of it – at the very onset of the rut. Once again, that's fairly typical of red deer behaviour. A quick sorting out of the men from the boys. In this case at least one of the boys appears to have given a very creditable account of himself. Despite the fact that CSM Markham was armed with a chair, Lance-Corporal Mason gored him in the ribs. The chairs, with which both were equipped were, interestingly enough, instinctively selected by the contestants as substitute antlers. With or without a chair, however, I would rank Markham as at least a 12-pointer. Observing his behaviour in the field, especially his courage and persistence in sneaking away hinds from the dominant stag's harem, I am even tempted to compare him to an Imperial, a 14-pointer. Remember, too, that he is still recovering from an early injury inflicted by Lance-Corporal Mason.'

'If Markham's an Imperial, what does that make Hulke?' Graham demanded.

'I shall come to Hulke in a moment. Meantime, Pomona is a fascinating case. I was at first inclined to write him off as a 12-pointer past his best and "going back" as we say. Shot his bolt in seasons past, no longer acceptable as prime breeding stock. However his appearance at Hind camp on the morning we landed there; his subsequent rutting behaviour; the fact that I have twice watched him engage CSM Markham, inconclusively as it turned out, in the parallel walk, which, as we all know often precedes an antler-to-antler confrontation: all these things suggest that his rutting days are by no means over, rather that he suffers some psychological check, a hang-over, if you like, from the pre-radiation period when his hormones were behaving in a normal human fashion. It is obvious that the radioactive exposure has affected different individuals to different degrees. My suggestion, therefore, is that Captain Pomona is inhibited from behaving in the role of master stag, for which his military rank obviously fits him, by his military training as a regular officer. In other words nine times out of ten, when he is tempted to fix antlers and charge, Queens Regs and a Sandhurst background order: "As you were . . ."

'Roxborough's a fascinating case, too. He appears to want to lek with the cocks and butt with the stags. Since I start with considerable previous knowledge of his make-up, I am frankly not surprised.' Sir Irwin turned to Janet. 'No doubt you have found, my dear, that Dr Roxborough has paid you considerable attention, little compliments, attempts to get you alone in the dark-room. That kind of thing.'

Janet nodded. 'I was quite able to deal with him.'

'I'm sure.' Sir Irwin smiled knowingly. 'But then Fergus, in many people's view, has always been one of those self-promoted ladies' men, mostly smoke and very little fire, if you know what I mean . . . So I find it quite in keeping with his previous sexual record that he shouldn't quite know where he's going. Most of the time he appears to believe he's a blackcock, probably because he thinks he looks rather good dressed up as Young Lochinvar. Fergus has always been terribly vain. Then occasionally, he turns up in tweeds and a deer-stalker at the rutting ground and gets chased off by Markham or Hulke.'

'What about Hulke?' Graham insisted. He was dying to hear Sir Irwin's theories about Hulke.

'Ah, Hulke. I have known Hammond Hulke for some time, too. He's an excellent field worker with a very wide knowledge of deer. However, he's not what you might call one of Nature's gentlemen, not to put too fine a point on it.' Sir Irwin paused to extract the most from the *mot* he was about to deliver. 'The point is: just *how* many points does Hammond Hulke put on it – on his head I mean. What do you say, MacCallister?'

'He's obviously *the* Master Stag, Sir Irwin. The Monarch of the Glen. He's chased off or beaten up every potential rival, even Markham. From all you say, he's almost certainly covered every hind on Horn. He must be at least an Imperial.'

'Must he, indeed? Notice anything special about the way Hulke attacks a rival?'

'Only that he used tremendous blundering force. More a kind of barge than a charge.'

'So what does that suggest?'

'That he doesn't favour a head-on clash.'

'Very good, MacCallister, as far as it goes, but it doesn't go quite far enough.'

'Perhaps he hasn't got quite such good antlers as we think . . .'

Sir Irwin faced his audience. 'The real truth is that Hulke doesn't have any antlers at all, real or imaginary.'

The light came to Graham in a great forked flash. 'He's a hummel,' he shouted.

Sir Irwin allowed a moment's irritation to pass over his face like a fleeting cloud shadow. Graham had pinched his pay-off line. Then the sun came out again. It was annoying, but if he waited a second, someone in the audience would feed him his cue. Raymond Braithwaite did so.

'And what, if I may ask, exactly is a hummel?'

'A hummel is the most dangerous and dreaded beast of all.'

'Without antlers?'

'Precisely. He's called a hummel, or humble, just because he has no antlers. But it's a complete misnomer. All the energy and food a normal stag puts into growing a bigger and better array of horn each summer, the hummel converts into flesh, bone and muscle. Haven't you noticed the enormous breadth of Hulke's shoulders, the depth of the chest?'

'He's always been a big lad,' mused Graham.

'I agree. A sort of human hummel, you could say. But the effects of the Dundoom leak have turned him into a positive monster, a living battering ram.'

Braithwaite asked: 'You mean a real hummel defeats the other stags equipped with conventional armament?'

'Most certainly I do. He turns and charges from the flank. His enormous strength and the confidence in the sheer brute power that goes with it can make a Royal or even an Imperial back down.'

'It certainly fits the facts of the case,' Graham admitted with admiration. Even Raymond Braithwaite was impressed.

'So a hummel is very likely to impregnate a great number of hinds?'

'Undoubtedly.'

'He could therefore sire a number of equally hornless male progeny?'

'Genetically it's possible, even probable.'

Janet said with feeling. 'What a dreadful thought. A lot of little Hulkes.'

'Of course, with a real hummel, something would have to be done about it.'

'What?' Braithwaite asked.

'Oh, for the good of the herd, he'd have to be taken out.'

'Taken out? Where?'

'Nowhere. A stalker would have to bump him off.'

A long moment of silence followed. Everyone appeared to be contemplating the obvious advantages of such a course.

'Out of the question, I suppose,' Braithwaite finally said sadly. 'He seems a pretty unpleasant sort of individual. He could mistake us for rivals and attack any of us.' He gestured at the still bemused Snettisham. 'We could end up like poor old Sniffy and he only tangled with CSM Markham, a mere 12-pointer. Someone will have to deal with Hulke eventually.'

'If the rut follows its normal pattern,' said Sir Irwin, 'he'll finally exhaust himself, though he's showing no sign of slowing down so far.'

'Meantime,' Braithwaite pointed out, 'it's high time we let the Prime Minister know something of our findings.'

'I agree. We must radio a message immediately. Something cryptic but which gives a clue to the real situation here.'

Braithwaite jumped up. 'I've got it. How about something like "Inhabitants of Horn appear to be in the rut?" That should tell him that something pretty unusual is going on.'

The *Haddie* had wandered a good deal during the past twelve hours. She had wandered through most points of the compass. She had wandered through, across, down, under and into the seas of which Cape Horn, let alone the Island of Horn, would have been proud. Finally, as the storm had moderated somewhat, she had wandered back on to her proper heading and pointed her bows towards the island again. It was at this point that she had wandered into the middle of the NATO exercise. For two hours, sleek grey shapes wearing the ensigns of the USA, of Holland, France, West Germany and the Scandinavian countries had loomed out of the spume and disappeared into it about their mysterious business and lawful occasions. Captain MacTavert's comments had in the main been intensely critical, critical of the seamanship of all concerned but critical in the main at a national level. Captain MacTavert, Nigel Newman concluded, did not approve of foreigners. He might, had there been one, just have spared a good word for the Scottish navy. Above all he most certainly did not approve of Russians and the trawler that suddenly appeared a mile astern of an American helicopter assault ship flaunted the Hammer and Sickle at her stern.

'Roosian bastards.'

'She's a spy ship,' said Nigel knowledgeably. 'They always send a trawler or two to observe NATO war games. It's quite legal. The high seas are international.'

'When I need you, laddie, to teach me maritime law, I'll

ask ye. To start wi', this is no' the high seas. These are Scottish territorial waters. Secondly, as far as I'm concerned, there's no legality about it. That Roosian's on my *Haddie*'s groonds. Thirdly, whatever else she's up to she's fushin! If ye cast yer eye over her stern, ye'll see the trawl cable.'

It was the longest speech Nigel had ever heard the Captain make. He was obviously deeply moved by the Russian trawler's presence. So, if the increased beat of its tired steel heart was anything to go by, was the *Haddie*. She was responding gallantly to Captain MacTavert's demands on her wheezing diesel for best speed. Encouraged by a following sea, she was rushing ahead surprisingly fast on what seemed to be a collision course.

'You're not going to ram her?' To Nigel it seemed highly possible. At the word 'ram', Ed the cameraman, prompted by some newsman's instinct that over-rode mere suffering, stuck his lime-coloured countenance up the companion-way leading from the *Haddie*'s tiny, fish-smelling cabin. He was clutching his camera. Gus the Grope followed, the chrome yellow of his features grotesquely framed by the earphones of his sound equipment.

'Good lads,' Nigel shouted. 'You'd better get a few close shots of this Russian. She's a spy trawler.'

Close shots presented no difficulty. Spinning the wheel as if trying to control a dodgem car on a skid-pan, MacTavert miraculously slid the *Haddie* under the Russian's counter, missing her by a coat of rust and taking her trawl wire on his bows to cut it neatly twenty feet from her propellors.

Nigel had a brief glimpse of an astonished bearded face gaping from the Russian's after deck. But his main impression was of the vast amount of electronic detection gear festooned about her upper works. None of it, he correctly surmised, was designed for detecting fish shoals.

MacTavert shook his fist at the fast-disappearing ship. 'That'll teach ye heathen Bolsheviks to fush in my pond.'

'Do you think he was really fishing?' Nigel asked.

'Nae doot, laddie. Did ye no see all those wireless gadgets? Those Roosians can spot a single herring at half a mile and have it inside a tin before ye can say Joe Stalin. It'll be quite a time before that skipper gets a new trawl streamed in this weather though. And they'll probably lock him up in the Kremlin for life for losing his gear and serve him bluidy well right.'

As they rose on the crest of the next huge sea, the Tine of Ben Dhui appeared briefly on the horizon.

'Four hours should do it the noo,' MacTavert announced happily. 'Have a dram, laddie.'

The PPS handed Sir Irwin Broadchalke's signal to the Prime Minister who read it slowly, held it up to the light as if it might contain a secret and more understandable message.

'Is it in code?' he asked at last.

'I don't think so, sir.'

'Did you ask them to repeat it?'

'They did so. It came over exactly the same.'

The Prime Minister read it out carefully. 'ALL CIVILIAN AND SERVICE PERSONNEL APPEAR TO BE RUTTING. BROADCHALKE.'

'I thought rutting was something deer did.'

'It is, sir.'

'Good God, man, do you mean that Ted Illingworth's diabolical gas has turned these innocent people into raving wild beasts?'

'A bit early to say, sir.'

'Why can't Broadchalke be more explicit?'

'You impressed on him the paramount need for secrecy.'

'Quite right. I did. Well, there's only one thing for it. He's got to make a report to me in person. Immediately! Get that chopper in to pick him up at once.'

'Fraid that's not possible. The Navy tell us that they've got something like a hurricane blowing up there. They expect it to last for at least three days before it moderates sufficiently to use a chopper.'

The Prime Minister sighed. 'Well at least that means no one else can get in or out of this damned island. We've got to keep this under wraps at all costs.'

Mavis Prendergast was beginning to feel that she had had

camping. She had also had, or to be more accurate, been had by Hammond Hulke. Five times. Then CSM Markham had cornered her twice. While as for MacGregor! MacGregor didn't bear thinking of. Sex, Mavis said to herself with more accuracy than she could possibly have imagined, was something she could do without for at least a year. She wriggled outside her survival tent. The undies she had washed in the burn and hung on a guy-rope to drip-dry overnight were frozen rigid. Survival, as far as Mavis and indeed most of the girls of Hind camp were concerned, was something that was becoming problematical.

Lieutenant Preece had come to the same conclusion. The time had come to wind up the training programme. Tomorrow she would march the girls back to the comfort and security of the Tracking Unit. Somewhere outside, Hulke was still bellowing his head off in defiance of a distant skirl of MacGregor's pipes. Myfanwy Preece experienced a moment of uneasiness. Would military discipline be able to withstand an all-out assault on her column of marching ladies? There were still those among her command who showed a partiality to Hulke's brand of sexual aggressiveness. The issue would have to be put to the test, that was all. She called Private Cassidy and ordered the cooks to prepare bag rations for next morning.

'Where are we going, ma'am?'

'For a route march.' Myfanwy saw no reason to give her plan away. Some of the girls might take fright.

Hulke roared again.

'What about him?' Private Cassidy asked. 'I mean: he's not going to like us going.'

'I'm in command here.'

'Oh, I see. Yes, I suppose so.' Private Cassidy sounded as though this idea hadn't occurred to her for some time.

In the past twenty-four hours, Graham had become increasingly worried about Janet. She had taken to returning late from field trips with Sir Irwin, seeming to want to linger alone on the hill. Back at NERTS headquarters she appeared to Graham to wear a preoccupied look, losing concentration during their discussions of the day's developments and staring out of the window towards the purple and brown braes of Ben Dhui. When, on several occasions, she had caught the distant sounds of stags roaring – or was it Hulke or possibly Markham? – she seemed, and Graham winced at the phrase, to be pricking up her ears. Was she, however slightly, however lightly, affected by the radiation? Was she coming in to a mild state of *oestrus*? If so, what of himself? As far as he was aware, he had experienced no further staglike symptoms. His voice had not deepened. He felt no thickening of the neck muscles. The dual points on his scalp no longer tingled. There was not the tiniest tintinnabulation in the ears. He seemed to be normal. More's the pity. If the worst was happening to Janet then she was likely to turn to the nearest dominant stag. Graham toyed with the idea of putting on a suitable display. Perhaps if he rolled in the peat bog behind Flora Flodden's cottage, or stood on the table and roared at Sir Irwin, or butted poor old Sniffy during one of this increasingly rare periods of lucidity, Janet might just take him for a master stag. His knowledge of red deer biology prompted him to doubt this. With the innate and very special sexual awareness of a hind in *oestrus* Janet would know he was simply putting on an act. *Oestrus* in red deer hinds had, Graham reflected bitterly, been her special study. What had he to pit against such knowledge? An analysis of faecal pellets, not much use in these or, for that matter, any other circumstances!

Raymond Braithwaite appeared from the direction of Janet's quarters.

'Seen the divine Morgan, Graham?'

'She's out on the hill with Sir Irwin.'

'Sir Irwin's been back half an hour.'

'Oh Christ!'

'Why so concerned?'

'I don't like her out there alone with Hulke on the loose.'

'In which case, shouldn't you go out to protect her?'

'Why me?'

'Oh nothing. I thought you were rather taken with her, that's all.'

'Are you suggesting that I might want to challenge Hulke to a rutting fight?'

'I have to keep an eye on you both. After all you *were* both lightly exposed.'

'Well, I assure you I'm normal.'

'Yes, I'm sure you are.'

'I don't like these innuendos about Janet. I say: *you* don't think she's showing symptoms?'

'No more than you think so, Graham.'

'Well, I don't. Janet's an experienced field worker. If she wants to spend an hour or two observing on her own . . .'

'Quite. Still, it's my job to check on all of us. If you see her, would you mind telling her I want to make a few more tests?'

'That's the second time in twenty-four hours.'

'Oh, and I'd better run the rule over you, too, Graham.'

Half an hour later, Janet returned to base. She was red-faced and out of breath. Graham noticed that her legs were scratched as if she'd been running through the heather.

Beneath a red October dawn, the *Haddie* was at last running under the grudging shelter of Horn.

Captain MacTavert took his breakfast, neat, out of the now familiar stone jar.

'Ye'll be glad to get ashore, nae doot.'

'Nae bluidy doot,' said Nigel.

'I'm no staying longer than it takes tae offload ma' cargo. When this wee breeze blows itself oot, the codling will be running if that Roosian hasn't swept the Scottish Ocean clear of fish.'

'You've got to wait to take us off again.'

'How long do you expect to be making your television show?'

'It's only a news item, not a bloody musical spectacular. There may be nothing in it.'

'Verra likely. There's nothing to be seen on Horn except deer and a few Army lassies.'

'That's not what I heard. We may want to stay a whole day.'

'Impossible. I'll be awa' this afternoon.'

'How much?' asked Nigel.

'One hundred poonds.'

'Oh, come off it. You only charged us a tenner each to get here.'

'Getting back from Horn is harder than getting to it.'

Nigel looked up at the lowering black shape of Ben Dhui. 'I can see that. Fifty then. Eighty all told. And you'll wait until four p.m.'

'Three p.m. I want to be clear of the Race of Horn before nightfall.'

'Okay. It's a deal.'

'Have a dram on it.'

Nigel swallowed the amber liquid gratefully. He hadn't felt as nervous as this since jumping with Rhodesian paratroopers into Mozambique.

Gus the Grope stuck his head up through the hatch and regarded the approaching hostile coast.

'Is that it?'

'Yes.'

'I think I'll just stay aboard and play a little deck tennis. You'll have to cover this story, mute, Nige.'

'Get your cans on, Gus. Any moment now we're going to hit the beach and from what I hear the natives may not be friendly.'

Captain MacTavert had somehow coaxed the *Haddie*'s bows towards what seemed to be an unbroken wall of rock. At the last moment he spun the wheel for a sharp turn to port. Ahead lay the hidden entrance to the little harbour and the first calm water they had seen since leaving the mainland over forty-eight hours previously.

About the time the *Haddie* put into harbour, the lek at Blackcock Camp was finally breaking up. MacGregor hadn't been around for a couple of days. Roxborough had put in one furtive appearance yesterday and had only then displayed half-heartedly in a pansified version of the Dashing White Sergeant. He'd hardly set to any of the still available hens and had eventually made off into the heather with a far from stylish *pas de Basque*. Under the direction of Corporal Dunfee and Jeannie McCall, tents were being struck, haversacks packed in preparation for the march back to camp.

Dr Jerry Mathews sat moodily by himself. Ever since his first disastrous appearance at the lekking ground, he hadn't felt part of things. He achieved very little success with the Scottish hens and none at all with Joanna Bromley. He watched Joanna sadly as she helped to pack up the gear, laughing and joking with the Army girls almost as if she'd taken the Queen's Shilling. Joanna was really behaving very strangely. She seemed to have forgotten that she was a scientist. She had even announced that she intended to march back to base with the Army instead of returning to NERTS HQ with him.

Jerry found it extremely difficult to be clear-headed. Though he had been compelled by some unfamiliar inner force to take part in the blackcock rituals, part of him had remained detached, realising what was happening while being powerless to alter or influence events. He had spent too much time studying blackcock not to know that he and his companions had been behaving exactly like them.

During the hectic days of lekking, most male blackcock had passed the long hours between the dawn and dusk display periods drinking, eating and sleeping in the widely spaced scattering of tents which served them as a camp. Even away from the lekking ground, none of the males could stand close proximity with his fellows. Because of his low dominance rating, Jerry had been forced to pitch his tent on the outside perimeter of the encampment. Partly out of fear that he would be assaulted, but largely out of boredom and lack of companionship, he had passed the daylight hours wandering the heather for all the world like a solitary and rejected non-breeding cock. In his wanderings he had witnessed some weird and, at the time, inexplicable events. He had, for instance, watched the arrival of the chopper and the rout of its three bowler-hatted occupants. He had lain in the heather above Hind Camp and observed the encounters between Hulke, Markham and Captain Pomona, to name but a few. An accomplished stalker, he had trailed Sir Irwin Broadchalke and Janet Morgan without being detected, and come to the correct conclusion that he was observing a pair of observers. But the activities that had intrigued him most were those of Graham MacCallister. Using his birdwatching binoculars, Jerry Mathews had eventually made out the nature of the instrument which Graham used so assiduously. On one occasion, he had looked right down from a crag on Graham working in a corrie fifty feet below him. He was close enough to hear the rapid series of clicks emitted by the instrument. His suspicion was fully confirmed. Graham was taking Geiger-counter readings of some unknown and previously unsuspected radiation. What's more, if the clicks were anything to go by, he was most assuredly getting those readings.

None of this made a great deal of sense – as yet. Nevertheless Jerry Mathews retained a confused conviction that all these events were in some way connected.

Corporal Dunfee was falling his parade in for the march back to the Tracking Unit. Hunched on his rock, Jerry watched the marchers set off, the men straggling behind. Then he slowly packed his gear and began the trek back to the NERTS cottages.

Nigel Newman led his three-man ITN team ashore as soon as the *Haddie* touched the quayside. Instinct told him to bypass the cottages. Bad tactics to invite immediate opposition on the beachhead. Officialdom was likely to be entrenched there. The helicopter pilot had given him a sketch map of the area where the fighting seemed to be thickest. Nigel skirted the cottages and found a track fifty yards to their rear.

The ITN crew pressed on for a mile. Nigel had little difficulty in identifying the level space by the burn which the chopper pilot had described. The marks where tents had recently been pitched showed up clearly. Ted, the cameraman, gloomily raked over the ashes in the remains of the improvised oven.

'Moved out two days ago.' He was rather proud of his John Wayne imitation. 'Shouldn't wonder if they're over the Texas border by now.'

Gus the Grope triumphantly held up the clip from a suspender belt. 'They got squaws with them.'

'Hang on a minute,' said Ted the cameraman. 'I heard a strange roaring sound.'

'Probably a walrus,' said Gus. 'I could do with a walrus recording.' Gus switched on his recorder and announced for the benefit of his mike: 'Atmosphere track with walrus, Horn.'

'There they are,' Nigel announced, pointing to the slope. Half a mile away a small group of khaki figures had appeared. 'Get set up, Ted.'

'Light's diabolical.'

'Never mind, we'll need some establishers. Besides they're headed this way.'

'Hey, there's that walrus again.' Gus was sweeping his directional mike around. 'Funny it's on dry land, somewhere up by the soldiers.'

'Don't be a berk. They don't have walruses in Scotland,' Nigel told him. 'That's a stag.'

Ted was focusing a 300 mm lens on the approaching column. 'Hell, that's no stag making that din. It's a feller. He's rushing down the slope towards the troops.' Despite Ted's gloomy prediction about the light, the camera had started to whirr.

Nigel whipped out a pair of miniature Zeiss folding binoculars from his anorak pocket. 'You're right, by God. It's like the chopper pilot said. Chap in khaki. He's just sent a poor sod in a kilt arse over tit. What the devil are they all at? You on to them, Ted?'

'Too right, I am. Look at that old biddy striding out ahead just as if nothing was happening.'

Dr Whymper would not have been pleased with the description.

'There's a right dolly bird bringing up the rear.'

Myfanwy Preece might have been flattered. Ted had seen a lot of dolly birds through the viewfinder in his time.

'Chap in khaki's trying to head them off. I can see him quite well now. Seems to be a sergeant-major by his arm badge.'

'Good for the old biddy. She's marching straight on.'

'Cannon to right of them, cannon to left of them . . .'

'I can fill the screen with them on the 200,' Ted said. He swung lenses on the camera turret. '*Did* you see *that*? The big party in front just shoved that sergeant-major type right into the heather.'

'Now he's gone back to try to cut off the tail end of the column.'

'Let me have a look,' Gus said plaintively. 'You're hogging all the crumpet.'

'Don't worry, Gus,' Nigel told him. 'They're going to pass quite close.'

The marching column was straggling now so that both Markham and Roxborough, for it was the latter who wore the kilt, had more opportunity to isolate stragglers.

'What the hell are they up to?' Nigel demanded. 'Just let them carry on a bit farther and then we'll try to get some interviews.'

All thought of attempting to stop the column was banished a second later as the tweeded form of Hammond Hulke came barrelling up out of a gulley, flooring Roxborough with an almighty butt in the chest and, a few seconds later, causing CSM Markham to roar, this time with pain, as Hulke's shoulder struck the sergeant-major squarely in his damaged ribs. The column wound gallantly on over a ridge and out of sight.

'After them!' commanded Nigel.

It was Jerry Mathews's bad luck that his course from the disbanded Blackcock Camp took him directly across Dr Whymper's bows. He appeared suddenly over a ridge to find the marching column with Dr Whymper at its head fast bearing down on him. Jerry stopped to give a friendly wave. It was his fatal mistake. Hulke obviously took him for yet another and possibly more determined sneaky rutter. Preliminaries and warning niceties such as a bout of parallel walking just did not occur in Hulke's rutting repertoire. As Dr Whymper swerved aside to take her girls safely away from what appeared to her to be yet more undesirable male attention, Hulke's shoulder crashed into Jerry, knocking the breath out of him. This time Hulke was not content to leave his rival lying prone in the heather. Maddened by the sudden withdrawal of all available hinds, Hulke proceeded to put the boot in. To escape the worst of Hulke's fury, Jerry rolled himself over and over until he reached a runnel filled with soggy peat. He lay there, semi-conscious, with the black, cold water seeping soothingly into his clothing. At least it was preferable to the thud of Hulke's walking boots. After stamping on Jerry a couple of times, Hulke roared again and took off at a trot after the fast disappearing column of girls.

'I got all that,' the cameraman announced happily.

'Sounded great,' said Gus. 'One or two words Mary Whitehouse wouldn't like but we can lay the walrus calls over those.'

'Come on,' commanded Nigel, 'we've got to interview that character as soon as he regains consciousness.'

Ten minutes later, a peat-blackened Dr Mathews was sufficiently recovered to face Nigel Newman and the camera. Though Nigel remained convinced throughout the rambling and often incomprehensible interview that he was in touch with a partly deranged mind, there was enough good stuff in Jerry's ravings to persuade him that he had indeed got a scoop. The message came across clearly that the island had been affected by a mysterious dose of radioactivity. Jerry was at his most lucid about Graham's use of the Geiger counter. The bit about being compelled to behave like a blackcock was harder to take. Easier to believe was Jerry's insistence that most of the population of Horn had been taking part in a short but hectic rutting season. Hadn't he himself, the battered scientist insisted, been half killed before their very eyes by a berserk master stag?

'Radiation,' raved the wild-eyed Jerry, 'can do terrible things to your sex hormones. Tell the world what they have done to us. Eggs!' he shrieked. 'Just imagine if they all start laying eggs.'

With these final words, Jerry stumbled back the way he had come as if even this brief trip back into the world of normality had snapped his mind.

'Cut,' Nigel ordered as he disappeared over the brow.

'Is he round the twist?' Gus asked. 'Whoever heard of birds, I mean real birds, laying eggs?'

'What next, skipper?' the cameraman asked.

'Let's see if we can catch up with any more of them, then back to the ship and try to persuade old Barnacle Bill to sail as soon as possible.'

'Don't you want to interview the Geiger counter expert or Sir Irwin what's-it?'

'I think not. Properly edited that crazy man's story is going to blow the lid off something or someone. Tangle with Sir Irwin and Colonel Snettisham, or even the Army commander, and we may well find Whitehall trying to put an embargo on the story. I've got a feeling that we're on to something big.'

'Do you think there's any danger that I'll turn into a stag?' Gus wanted to know.

'Nae bother. You've been one all your natural. The only difference is you have a twelve-month rutting season.'

'Thank God for that.'

By the time Nigel and his men got back to the harbour Captain MacTavert had off-loaded his supplies by the simple expedient of heaving them off the *Haddie* on to the quayside. With the single exception of a crate containing malt whisky. This he had reverently carried ashore, extracting two bottles for himself as Customs duty.

'Seen anyone from the cottages?'

'Verra strange. They peeped at me from behind their curtains like a lot of auld women. The *Haddie* might just as well have been flying a yellow flag as if she had the plague aboard.'

'Perhaps *they've* got some sort of plague, here on the island.'

'Ah well, whisky's a powerful preventative against the plague. You'll all take a dram for safety's sake?'

MacTavert thoughtfully removed a third bottle from the opened crate.

'When can you sail?'

'As soon as you get yerselves aboard.'

Gus gazed fearfully out through the narrow entrance of

the harbour to where the Scottish Ocean waited ready, green and eager to pounce on the *Haddie*.

'Leave me here with a tin of ship's biscuits and a barrel of water,' he pleaded.

'Awa' wi' ye,' the captain told him. 'The sea's moderated fine. It's barely Force Six, the noo.'

An hour after the *Haddie* cleared the Race of Horn, the Russian spy trawler *Kara* made the shelter of the island. Her captain had had a hard time making the landfall. The trawl-line which MacTavert had so skilfully cut had caught round the *Kara*'s stern-post giving the skipper about a quarter of the normal manoeuvrability on his rudder. A close study of that invaluable guide to international mariners, 'The British Pilot', had told him that there was, indeed, a tiny harbour on the east side of the island of Horn. If he could creep in there, steering largely with his twin screws, he would be able to put a diver over the side and clear the obstruction.

Captain Pomona stared listlessly out of his orderly-room window. Life had lost all spice for him recently. His unit was off the air. He felt no interest in anything. His troops were away somewhere under canvas on a lunatic training scheme ordered by the MOD and at least condoned by himself. His voice, which only a week or so ago had become surprisingly gruff, now showed a tendency to crack into the treble clef. He pined for the good old days when everybody under his command seemed to be obsessed with only one thing. Sex was the last thing *he* thought of now. He felt lonely and deserted. Even the company of Regina Whymper would have been welcome.

Pomona sat up suddenly. His ears had caught the sound of marching feet. He ran to the window just as Dr Regina Whymper, considerable chest thrown out, muscular arms swinging, came swaggering round the corner of the mess hut on to the parade ground. Behind her, in good order, except that their clothes and features suggested they had been engaged in a long period of hand-to-hand fighting, strode his gallant men, or rather women. In fact, not a single man marched with them. Pomona saw that the little column consisted of all the hens and hinds of Blackcock and Hind Camps. Somewhere along the trail, the two parties had got together. But where were the men?

Myfanwy Preece called the parade to a halt. The girls picked up their dressing. As to their personal dressing, there wasn't too much left to pick up. Some items, though only their owners knew which, had been discarded irretrievably out there on the rutting ground. For the rest, slacks were torn, lapels ripped, stockings and tights hanging in strips that resembled the work of a mad spider. There was, nevertheless, something about the detachment's bearing, a certain panache, a battle-seasoned jauntiness that suggested they had been through a great deal and come out, figuratively speaking at least, on top.

Lieutenant Preece addressed them: 'You have shown the men of this island what you are made of.'

'Mebbe once too often, I'm thinking,' muttered Jeannie McCall.

'You have responded beyond the call of duty. As a result of our time together under canvas, I think I can assure you that Army life will take on a new and more productive meaning. You will find you will have gained something precious by your service in the field.'

'I'm hoping not,' murmured Jeannie.

'From now on, we women will find a new bond. We have been tried, tested and tempered in the fires of experience.'

Captain Pomona blinked. Even for a Welshwoman this was an unexpected flight of oratory. It sounded to him dangerously like some brand of Women's Lib. Not at all like the Myfanwy he had known and loved.

'Hot baths and a new issue of clothing will be arranged for you all. Parade, dis-Miss.'

'Lieutenant Preece,' Captain Pomona called. Myfanwy approached and saluted smartly.

'Good afternoon, Lieutenant. Nice to see you back.'

'Sir!'

'Oh, do relax, Myfanwy.'

'Thank you, sir.'

'Please don't be so formal. Come in and have a chat.'

'Got to look after my girls, sir.'

'They're perfectly capable of looking after themselves from what I remember of them. Where are the men?'

'Men?' Myfanwy said this as though the unit had never included any.

'Yes, men, Myfanwy. You must remember them. Why only the other day . . .'

'They'll still be out on the hill, I imagine, sniffing around and roaring a bit. You did a pretty good roar yourself, sir.'

'Yes, well, thanks, but that's all over now.'

'Except for Hulke. He'll go on until he drops.'

The conversation was fast getting out of control, slipping back into a dreamtime from which Pomona felt he had escaped, hoped he had escaped. He made a supreme effort.

'As soon as CSM Markham and the rest return, we'll get back to normal. I intend to ask MOD for permission to put the Tracking Unit back on the air. We'll need a work-up programme, a short training period. I'll make out a joint manning roster as before.'

'Beg pardon, sir. Can't be done now. Not males and females in the same watches. My girls won't have anything to do with the men from now on. With respect, sir, we'll have to run the unit separately. The girls will insist on sticking together.'

Pomona shook his head as if shaking a malfunctioning watch in the hope of setting it ticking again.

'Thank you, Myfanwy. You go and have a nice hot soothing bath. Perhaps we can talk later.'

Next morning, Sir Irwin Broadchalke poked his head out of the front door and found himself face to face with the Hammer and Sickle. The red flag was flying at the stern of the *Kara*. He shut the door with a bang and called out: 'Snettisham. There's a Russian warship in the harbour.'

Snettisham walked shakily across the room and made an effort to focus his still-concussed pupils. At the sight of her the Colonel perked up. 'That's not a warship. She's a spy trawler. By God, she's got some lovely equipment. See that green metal disc rotating slowly above her bridge? That's a radioactive sensor. It can sniff out a nuclear warhead five miles away.'

'Why's it turning round now?' Sir Irwin demanded. 'None of the rest of the gubbins appears to be working. There aren't any nuclear warheads on Horn . . . Hey, wait a minute . . . Do you think? . . .'

Sniffy was positively ecstatic. He'd even forgotten he still had trouble seeing much less than quadruple.

'Of course, I *think*. With the apparatus she's got there, they could get a bleep out of old Graham's faecal pellets at a mile range. Oh, there's no doubt they've discovered we've had a dose of something nasty.'

'We ought to tell the Army.'

'I *am* the Army.'

'Shouldn't you do something about it?'

'What? Board them single-handed? She's probably manned by NKVD men all armed to the teeth.'

'Can't you tell them to shove off?'

'Wouldn't do much good. Besides, they're probably doing much less harm here than cruising around taking photographs of NATO battleships and annoying aircraft carriers. Besides, I might do a bit of spying myself.' The Colonel began absently to sketch the Russian's detection aerials on the table cloth.

After a minute, Sir Irwin said: 'Hey, look. They're lowering a frogman over the side. I bet they're up to no good. Remember that Buster Crabbe fellow? He was up to no good.'

'Supposed to be on our side.'

'Who? The Russians?'

'No. Crabbe. He got drowned.'

'I think I'll go outside and ask them just what the devil they think they're doing.'

Having made the decision, Sir Irwin felt himself suddenly defenceless. The remains of his bowler hat and neatly rolled umbrella were hanging behind the door. Perhaps because he saw them as the only possible emblems with which to answer the Hammer and Sickle, he put his ruined bowler on and stepped out of the cottage carrying his brolly at the high port.

A ship's officer in a fur cap was leaning over the stern rail staring down at the stream of bubbles rising from the now submerged diver.

'I say. Good morning. What exactly do you chaps think you're doing in our harbour?'

The Russian had obviously, at some point in his life, been exposed to the culture of the West. Smiling broadly he made a gesture whose message was unambiguous.

Sir Irwin retired to the cottage to think this over. At one level, he had found it rather heart-warming that he and the Russian thus far spoke a common language. Nevertheless, he had, unmistakably, been told to mind his own business.

Ten minutes later, when Sniffy Snettisham had fallen into a state of semi-coma once again and Sir Irwin was demolishing his third slice of toast and marmalade, two figures in parkas and fur hats descended the *Kara*'s gangplank and set off inland bearing electronic equipment which Colonel Snettisham would no doubt have identified had he been fully present upon the current scene.

After his encounter with the ITN crew Dr Jerry Mathews decided not, after all, to return to NERTS HQ. He had spent a cold and disturbed night in his tent. He made himself breakfast from an opened crate of emergency rations and then, since he had no particular purpose in life any more, decided to wander about in the heather.

The two figures in dark blue parkas were obviously scientists. He deduced this because they were using scientific equipment. One was engaged in a pursuit that was well-known to him. He was taking soil, rock, and vegetation samples and enclosing them in labelled plastic bags. It was the sort of thing scientists did more or less compulsively all the time all over the world. The other man was using electronic apparatus with a portable aerial of a kind unfamiliar to him. Jerry did not recognise either man. Their blue parkas suggested that they were Navy personnel. This seemed highly likely since from high up on Ben Dhui, he had noticed warships recently steaming about off Horn. Come to think of it, he recalled someone saying ages ago that a large NATO exercise was due to take place in these waters. Jerry hailed the nearer of the two, the soil sampler.

The man who had a beard and a large flat friendly face looked up. 'Hello,' he said in a musical foreign accent. 'Good day. How are you?'

'You Navy?'

The man nodded.

'Part of the NATO exercise?'

'*Da*,' said the other man with the electronic gear.

'Swedish?' asked Jerry in a moment of linguistic inspiration. The word '*Da*' had given him a clue.

'That's right,' the bearded spokesman agreed. 'Swedish scientists.'

'I'm a scientist, too.'

'We are colleagues then. The great brotherhood of science. It crosses international boundaries.'

'Absolutely right, old boy. Things have been very odd here lately. Glad someone else has spotted it.'

'So. Perhaps, in the name of science, we should put our findings together.'

Jerry pointed at the electronic apparatus. He could see a needle flickering frantically.

'Radiation detector?'

'Excuse me?'

'Oh come on. You can't fool me. We're on to it, too.'

'Indeed.'

'I forget when it started.'

'When what started?' asked the soil sampler gently.

Jerry put his finger to his lips for silence. They listened. An outraged roar echoed across the hills.

'*That* started.'

'Deer! We have deer in Rus . . . in Sweden, too.'

'Not a deer,' said Jerry. 'That's Hulke.' Something like terror had entered his eyes and the Russian had spotted it.

'Sit down. There's nothing to be afraid of. What is this Hulke?'

'A man. A madman. Behaving like a stag. That's his rutting roar. Ever since . . . ever since . . .'

'Ever since what?'

'The Highland dancing.'

'Please explain Highland dancing.'

'I can't. Nobody can. But that's when it all started.'

'Very interesting. Perhaps an outside scientific opinion . . . Why don't you tell me about it?'

Talking to this large, friendly Swedish scientist was almost as good as confessing to a priest. As far as he was able, Jerry proceeded to give this large friendly Swedish scientist a first-hand account of the only rutting season so far known in the history of mankind.

Hulke was by no means done yet. MacGregor was a menace to his superiority. MacGregor must be subdued so long as there was a single hind left on Horn to be covered. The fact that he hadn't sighted a hind all day was doing little for Hulke's throbbing gonads. Even more roar-provoking was MacGregor's continual challenge to his, Hulke's, undoubted dominance in a manner which Hulke found impossible to counter. All morning long, MacGregor had been roaring round on that abominable, stinking machine, making false charges to within yards and then swerving away before Hulke could catch him and bowl him over.

Something about the shape of MacGregor's mechanical aid was so infuriating. Here the Scots bastard came again. Hulke glared at the bouncing, snarling Greaves scrambler. It was those handlebars, upswept and aggressive like the horns of a well-endowed stag that maddened him. He, Hulke, didn't need such assistance. MacGregor swerved within feet of Hulke. Then, because he was low on petrol and had no wish to be caught by Hulke, unmounted, he headed back towards the cottages to top up his tank.

Hulke watched him go. Very well, if MacGregor insisted on challenging him on two wheels, he would return that challenge on four. He began to walk back to where he had hidden his Land-Rover.

MacGregor was enjoying himself enormously. He had never liked Hulke. He filled his tank with a light heart and rode off to conduct another harassing action. The Anzani engine roared its message of speed and power. MacGregor whooped at the thought that Hulke must hear him coming.

Hulke, in fact, did not hear him coming for the simple

reason that he was himself encased in an even more smothering cocoon of automotive cacophony. A Land-Rover is not, at the best of times, a silent conveyance. The fact that his Land-Rover had lost its silencer added both to the din and to his enjoyment. Thus, vengeance uppermost in both their skulls, twelve-pointer and hummel advanced upon each other, down the same narrow track and, rounding a bend, came upon each other at a pace and fury never equalled by any pair of rutting stags.

There was no place to which Hulke could safely swerve without risk of instant disintegration against a rock. Not so MacGregor, however. With his far greater manoeuvrability he could have easily turned aside into the heather. Instead he opened the throttle to its widest extent. He would give Hulke a fright that would surely send him skulking away, defeated. A large flat, upward-sloping boulder lay at mid-point between Land-Rover and Greaves. MacGregor was adept at jumping the scrambler over large obstructions. Now he judged that if he could only attain enough speed in the few seconds left, he could heave back on the handlebars, causing the Greaves to jump over Hulke's windscreen. And so he might have done had not Hulke applied his brakes at the last moment. It could be argued that in causing Hulke to do this, MacGregor had won the moral victory he sought. The effect was catastrophic. MacGregor's leap more than matched that made by his famous ancestor Rob Roy across the gorge of the River Lyon.

Instead of clearing the Land-Rover, he landed squarely on its roof, bounced once, performed a somersault in the air, parted company with the Greaves and landed in a peat bog. Hulke did not stop to look back. Had he done so he would have been extremely gratified. MacGregor had disappeared. Only his tartan cap rose above the ooze. The shattered Greaves smoked sulkily in the heather; the hated handlebars had parted company with the parent body, looking exactly like the shed antlers of a stag.

Jerry Mathews had enjoyed his chat with the friendly Swedish scientist. The bearded man had been fascinated by everything Jerry had to tell him. They'd got on so well that Jerry had accepted an invitation to visit him aboard his ship to compare notes.

Jerry had barely a mile to cover to the harbour when he caught the sound of the Land-Rover approaching fast up the track behind him. Hammond Hulke came round a bend to see Jerry ambling along a hundred yards ahead. Jerry turned and jerked his thumb to request a lift. Hulke's reply was to jam his foot hard down and drive straight at his target. As Jerry sprang aside, he had a close view of the set features of Hulke staring fixedly through the screen as he tore crazily onwards.

Jerry was taking no more chances. Over the hill he could see the masts of the trawler. He would walk across country to the harbour. The sooner he reached the sanctuary of the ship the better. The Swedes might even be persuaded to take him to the mainland.

Sir Irwin was watching the Russian trawler from the parlour window.

'You're a bit of a sailor aren't you, Braithwaite?'

'Got a cruiser on moorings at Chichester, if that's what you mean.'

Sir Irwin pointed at the trawler's stern.

'What's that diver chap taking down with him?'

'Underwater cutting gear. Oxy-acetylene torch, I think.'

'What do you think's wrong?'

'Probably got something caught round her propellors. Steel cable maybe.'

'That why they came in here, do you imagine?'

'Maybe.'

'Not to spy on us?' Sir Irwin sounded relieved. 'You don't think they know anything about the leak?'

'No. Why should they?'

'Sniffy says . . .'

'Sniffy's half bonkers since he got that crack on the head.'

An hour later Sir Irwin called out: 'Smoke's coming out of her funnel. I think she's getting ready to shove off.'

As the man at the bows stood by the forward mooring

cable, Dr Jerry Mathews appeared running wild-eyed up the street towards the Harbour. He had just reached the jetty when the NERTS Land-Rover hurtled, headlights blazing and horn blaring, round the corner behind him.

'Good God. It's Hulke.'

'He's going to knock the poor sod into the sea.'

The gap between the *Kara* and the quayside was beginning to widen as Jerry leapt. He would not have made it had not a bearded figure in a blue parka stretched out a welcoming hand.

Frustrated but apparently satisfied, Hulke backed off and roared away past the cottages out of sight.

The *Kara* cleared the mouth of the harbour and headed out to sea.

'They've kidnapped poor old Mathews.'

'You could say he defected.'

'I say. Did you notice Hulke?'

'One could hardly miss him.'

'I mean his behaviour. He's acting out of character. A hummel relies entirely on his own weight and strength. He doesn't need antlers. He was using that Land-Rover as substitute horns. He's getting pretty desperate!'

'Why's that?'

'No hinds around maybe.'

'That reminds me. Where's Janet?'

'Are you worried about her condition?'

'No . . . but she has shown an increasing tendency to wander recently. With Hulke in that state, she'll have to watch herself.'

'Hulke's turning very nasty. It's the end of the rut . . .' Sir Irwin paused. 'The Prime Minister will have to be told.'

'About Hulke?'

'Don't be bloody silly. That can wait. He has to know that the Russians have snatched one of my staff.'

On the rare occasions that the Prime Minister escaped from the House early he liked to catch the news on the box. To compare degrees of what he called distortion and unfair bias, he tried to watch the BBC and ITV alternately, though he sometimes cheated. When he did so, Anna Ford's heart-shaped innocence won by a rounded vowel over Angela Rippon's suggestion that nannie could be kind as well as severe. This evening he was in the mood for Anna. 'News at Ten' was halfway through. A government commercial for saving energy was just ending. He must ask Ted Illingworth how much he was spending on a campaign that invited public-spirited viewers to turn off the lights when they left the room. Bloody silly slogan: 'The meter doesn't know when you're not there . . .'

As he switched on, Anna was saying: 'On a remote island off the coast of North-West Scotland, ITN reporter Nigel Newman has discovered that something very strange indeed is going on.'

The Prime Minister relaxed. This was going to be one of those nice off-beat items the ITN boys did so well. Probably about some weird Caledonian local custom. A second later he experienced the sort of shock that might have been caused had all the amps and volts saved by Ted Illingworth's switch-off-more-lights campaign been re-routed through the seat of his chair.

'This is Nigel Newman on an island seventy-five miles off the north-west Scottish coast. The island is called Horn.'

The Prime Minister leapt up and adjusted all the controls at once with the result that Nigel came through louder, clearer and in even brighter colour.

'Today I witnessed the most extraordinary behaviour on the part of the Army detachment and civilian scientists stationed on Horn.'

Pop-eyed with horror, the Prime Minister watched the column of marching girls, led by Dr Whymper, striding down the heather-covered slope. He heard the whoops and shrieks, the strangled oaths as a kilted figure attacked the column. There was even a sound that made him think of a walrus barking. The kilted man was driven off by a burly warrant officer until both were finally routed by a maniac in tweeds.

Newman was talking to camera again. 'A few seconds later, the tweeded figure, who turned out to be a well-known scientist studying deer on Horn, attacked and severely mauled a third victim . . .'

Gripping the arms of his chair, the Prime Minister watched as Hulke kicked the unfortunate Jerry as he lay in the peat bog.

'A few moments later, I was able to interview this victim, another scientist, Dr Jerry Mathews, and this is what I learned.'

Jerry's semi-incoherent ravings had been skilfully edited with reverses of Newman looking incredulous and even cutaways of rutting deer and lekking blackcock hastily obtained from *Survival*'s library of natural history film. It became very clear that the aggressive behaviour that the viewers had just witnessed was part of a human rutting season that had affected every living person on Horn, even Dr Mathews.

'I found myself behaving exactly like a randy blackcock,' Mathews was saying.

The Prime Minister averted his eyes, thinking simultaneously of Mary Whitehouse and the Race Relations Act. His features matched the cover of a White Paper on energy conservation that lay before him on his desk. He felt as blue as the jacket of the report on leaks from atomic power stations which he knew must surely follow.

Worse was to come.

Nigel Newman was asking: 'Can you suggest any explanation for this apparent conversion of people into wild beasts?'

The Prime Minister held his breath. How could this mad, dishevelled scientist have guessed unless Sir Irwin or one of his colleagues had sprung a leak as fatal as Dundoom's? Here it came.

'People,' said Dr Mathews, 'have been taking Geiger counter readings. I've watched them. Those readings have been very definitely positive, showing a high degree of radiation. Radiation can do terrible things to one's hormones.'

It was Jerry's final line before he rushed away like a tortured soul into the heather that shook the Prime Minister most of all.

'Just imagine,' Jerry was saying, 'if all those women started laying eggs.'

Nigel Newman was winding up to camera.

'I would have found it hard to believe Dr Mathews's strange story if I hadn't watched the stag-like behaviour of those three aggressive males with my own eyes. And if there is something in his story about excessive radiation, where did it come from? From outer space? From atomic waste dumped in the ocean? From an H-bomb test in the Soviet Union or from a leak from one of our own atomic power stations? The last explanation seems the most likely but the nearest nuclear power station is seventy-five miles away on the mainland at Dundoom. This is Nigel Newman, News at Ten, on the, perhaps, too aptly named island of Horn.'

The phone rang just as the Prime Minister was picking it up to call his PPS.

'Prime Minister,' said his PPS, 'the MOD has just passed us a message from Horn.'

'You can't tell me anything. I've just seen "News at Ten". I want an emergency meeting here at once. Illingworth, the Minister for Health, the press secretary. Within half an hour. We'd better have that Brigadier, too.'

'What about the Navy, sir?'

'Why the hell should I want the Navy?'

'Perhaps I should give you the message, sir. It reads: "NERTS scientist Dr Jerry Mathews sailed on Russian spy trawler KARA. Suspect he is mentally disturbed but he may have defected. Either way must emphasise his presence aboard KARA constitutes a grave security risk. Signed Broadchalke."'

'Mathews is the chap I just saw on the telly. I'll say he's a security risk. We'll have to sink her.'

'That may be a bit drastic, sir.'

'I'll decide that.'

'Quite, sir. You'd like the Navy to attend then, Prime Minister?'

'I was about to say that. Get the First Sea Lord. And phone the press secretary at once. Tell him I want a stop put on the Horn story.'

'The press won't like that. Nor will ITN.'

'Cover them with "D" notices.'

'But surely the story's out now?'

'Then ITN must be told to put out a late night bulletin persuading the viewers it was all a hoax.'

'They won't like that either, sir.'

'No? And the public won't like the thought that they might all be turned into stags – or blackcock. Imagine the effect that might have in Brixton.'

An hour later, across the Cabinet table, the Prime Minister faced the Ministers for Energy and Health, the Press Secretary, the First Sea Lord and the Brigadier commanding Tracking Stations, Scotland.

'There's no doubt,' he said, 'we have a grave crisis at both a national and international level. Let us deal with the international aspects first. A British scientist in possession of highly classified nuclear information has fallen into Russian hands. This spy ship . . . the . . .'

'*Kara*, Prime Minister,' said the First Lord. 'She's well known to us. Hangs around every fleet exercise like a dog around a bitch on heat.'

The Prime Minister winced at the reference, however oblique, to animal mating procedures. He wished Admirals weren't so salty.

'She's decorated with electronic detection devices like a Christmas tree. Pretty sophisticated stuff, especially on radiation.'

The Prime Minister groaned. 'Then she must be sunk. Rammed by a destroyer. God, there are enough NATO ships up there. They're always ramming something when they're not meant to.'

The First Lord smiled. 'I'm afraid the Russians might not take kindly to the idea. We happen to know they've got five nuclear subs in the area.'

'Then board her. Remember the *Altmark*.'

'I seem to recall we were at war then, Prime Minister. We could request them to transfer Dr Mathews to us at sea.'

'Request! What's the Royal Navy coming to?'

'Perhaps we could exchange him,' suggested the Brigadier.

'By then it will be far too late. They'll have got all they want to know out of him.'

'Assuming there's anything *to* get,' Ted Illingworth, Minister for Energy, sounded hopeful.

'Of course there's something to get. Imagine what *Pravda* would make out of the Atomic Energy Commission ruining innocent citizens' sex lives.'

The meeting digested the international implications of this gravely, without really seeing what business it was of the Russians or anyone else if Britain chose to upset twenty-seven sets of its own nationals' hormones.

After a longish pause, the Prime Minister said: 'I want Broadchalke and those other two chaps I sent to Horn flown here immediately.'

'Weather's easing up,' said the First Sea Lord. 'We might get a chopper in for them tomorrow.'

'Good. You sure you can't accidentally sink that Russki?'

''Fraid it's out of the question Prime Minister.'

'And another thing. I want a state of blockade imposed on Horn. No one's to get in or out, by air or by sea.'

'I think I can guarantee that, Prime Minister.'

'Good. There's been enough leaking on Horn so far to sink the bloody island and maybe that's not such a bad idea.'

Early next morning, Lance Corporal Mason delivered a message at the NERTS cottages. Sir Irwin read it out: 'Conditions permitting, Sir Irwin Broadchalke, Dr Braithwaite and Colonel Snettisham are to stand by for helicopter pick-up from 1000 hours. Signed Fairfax, Capt. RN, HMS Greylag.'

'What's the *Greylag*?' Sir Irwin wanted to know.

'She's a goose class chopper assault ship,' the Colonel told him. He appeared to possess a surprising number of his marbles for this hour of the morning. Possibly his condition was at last improving.

'Big?' Sir Irwin asked hopefully.

'Small,' the Colonel said.

Sir Irwin looked prematurely green. He wasn't a very good sailor. He cheered up as a thought struck him.

'Not that we'll be aboard her long, I imagine. This signal can only have come from the Prime Minister. With luck, we'll be back in London by tonight.'

Graham said: 'We're going to miss you chaps, after all we've been through together.'

'Don't worry, MacCallister. NERTS has a big problem on its hands here. You could call everything that's happened simply an extension of the red deer study programme. I've no doubt some of us will be back. Meantime you're to take charge of the study programme.'

'No more faecal pellets, Sir Irwin?'

'Drop them. For the time being.'

'Consider them dropped.'

'You and Dr Morgan will . . .'

Braithwaite interrupted: 'Oh by the way, Graham, there's something I want to tell you. Janet's last test, made late last night, is slightly unusual. It could reveal the onset of a very mild *oestrus*. On the other hand it might be part of the normal female cycle. I've suspected she might be on the brink for some days past. Don't worry too much, Graham. Janet's certainly not seriously affected like the rest of the girls. But keep an eye on her. Try to stop her straying, especially while Hulke's still on the prowl. I wouldn't like . . .'

'I wouldn't like either. Where *is* Janet, by the way?'

'She hasn't come down to breakfast.'

Graham jumped up and ran to the next-door cottage. Pinned to Janet's door was a note.

'Got up early. Gone to do some post-rut hind observations high up on Ben Dhui. Back mid-morning.'

Graham was halfway back to his own cottage when he heard Hulke's Land-Rover revving furiously in the distance. Now he really was alarmed. If Hulke was on the prowl this early then Janet was certainly in danger. Had Hulke spotted her setting off up the track towards Ben Dhui and started in pursuit?

Graham seized his binoculars and anorak from behind

the cottage door. By taking the sheep track across the high ground it should still be possible to reach Janet before Hulke did.

But Graham had reckoned without the determination and drive of a frustrated master stag – and a hummel at that. As he climbed higher along the narrow track he saw that Hulke had not parked his Land-Rover by the shearing shed where the vehicle track normally ended. Instead he was forcing it in bone-shaking fits and juddering starts, directly up the mountain in a zig-zag route through the heather. Hulke was not making much speed but he was staying ahead in the race to reach Janet. Graham could see her walking at an unhurried pace up the track which she always used to reach her favourite hind observation ground below the Tine.

Graham could go no faster. Far ahead he saw the pale flash of Janet's face. She had stopped and looked back. Perhaps she had at last caught the sound of pursuit. Graham consoled himself that Janet knew all about Hulke and what was likely to happen if he caught up with her. But then a terrible thought struck him. Supposing Raymond Braithwaite's suspicions were justified? What, if as a result of a light dose of radiation, she was entering upon a delayed though mild state of *oestrus*? Might she not just possibly accept the brutish Hulke's even more brutish attentions? Graham paused for breath and to focus his binoculars. The sweet form and features of Janet appeared in the powerful glasses. She looked as tranquil and self-possessed as ever. Now that she was threatened, Graham's heart nearly burst for good old-fashioned human, heterosexual love for her. He drove himself onwards and upwards.

The tortured roar of the Land-Rover engine had stopped. Hulke had run it deep into a peat bog and there was the dismounted Hulke bounding straight up the mountainside towards Janet with the spring, speed and strength of the hummel which he so closely resembled.

A new sound struck Graham's tortured ears. The roaring of a master stag. Graham had no doubt from whom this sound originated. He could see Hulke throwing back his head to bell as he climbed.

This time Janet reacted. There was now panic in her gait as she stumbled upwards towards the rock wall at the foot of the Tine. Panic? Or was it evasiveness of the sort shown by red deer hinds when they mean to succumb to a rutting stag but not quite yet?

Graham's heart was hammering against his rib cage with the breathless pace of the climb. For the first time he felt hope. For some minutes past Hulke had disappeared from view. There was a perfectly natural explanation for this. He had entered a small corrie that lay between him and the Tine. Graham knew every inch of the ground there so he was puzzled. Hulke should have been through the corrie and well on his way towards Janet several minutes ago. Had he, with luck, fallen? Perhaps with even better luck he had broken a leg. The corrie was filled with jagged boulders and loose scree. Terrible stuff to cross when a man was in a hurry. Even stags sometimes made mistakes there.

More confident now, Graham paused for a second to catch his breath. As he did so, he heard a barrage of furious roaring. Hulke must have stopped to display there, no doubt to impress and intimidate Janet still further. Well, bad luck, Hammond Hulke!

When Graham broke out on the open ground below the Tine, Hulke had still not appeared from the corrie. Janet saw Graham and turned holding out her arms, as if for help. 'Wait!' he shouted. She pointed frantically downwards towards the corrie and he saw her lips form the word 'Hulke'.

'I know,' he shouted. 'Wait!'

This was not the self-possessed Janet he had always known. She was frightened, clawing her way along the base of the rock, looking up towards the peak as though the Tine alone could offer her safety.

'Wait, Janet!'

She was round the far side of the rock wall before he caught her. She was trembling like a thrush held in the hand.

'That man,' she said, 'that awful man.'

'You're safe with me.'

'Not from him! Up there.' She pointed to the Tine above

them. 'Where you sometimes go. He can never reach me there.'

'All right,' he said. 'Up there, then.'

Graham remembered the words MacGregor had used the night of the rutting full moon. 'A lassie could make the climb.'

'This way,' he said. 'I'll show you. Use the foot- and hand-holds as I tell you.'

Minutes later, a breathless Janet found herself facing the drain hole that led into the grass-lined cup on top of the Tine. 'Hang on,' Graham called. 'I'm going to help you through.' Janet felt herself propelled upward and forward on to a bed of soft mosses and sweet-smelling grass. Graham wriggled through and lay beside her.

'There,' he said, by way of announcing that she was safe and then soothingly as to a child he said: 'There, there!'

He smoothed her cheek.

She moved towards him.

'Lie there. You're safe now. You're with me.'

Janet half rose, listening. 'He's still at it,' she said, fear returning to her flecked green eyes.

It was true. Hulke was roaring loudly below in the corrie, making enough din for two master stags.

'Let's look,' Graham said. 'He can't possibly see us. Deer never look upwards for danger, remember?'

Together they peered cautiously over the rock lip of the Tine. From this vantage point they looked almost directly down into the corrie into which Hulke had disappeared. The reason for his non-reappearance was now very clear.

Two magnificent beasts faced each other in the corrie. On the lower ground stood Hulke, the human hummel. Twenty yards above him, Horn's 'Royal', the true monarch of its glen, a master stag as to the manner born, a 12-pointer in his prime, commanded the route to the Tine.

Hulke pawed the ground and roared louder than ever. The 12-pointer lowered his splendid head and thrashed the grass with his antlers. Hulke apparently had decided that this kind of exchange had gone on quite long enough. With a final roar he rushed up the slope. The 12-pointer had had enough, too. He might be giving away weight to his rival but he held the high ground. The 12-pointer saw Hulke coming and, allowing for a hummel's treacherous last-minute switch to a flanking attack, charged downhill, catching Hulke head-on. He lifted the human hummel high on his antlers, tossed him and, when he fell, butted and rolled him down the scree until he lay motionless and insensible at the bottom of the corrie. The Royal raised his head, roared triumphantly and trotted to the top of the corrie. There he almost seemed to pose, antlers outlined against the sky. He roared and roared again.

Janet sank back on to the grass.

'The natural order . . .' she said mysteriously.

'Yes, Janet. The natural order of things.'

'Hulke won't give any more trouble.'

'No. I think not. He's been deposed. For him, the rut is over.'

'For us it never even started.'

'Thank God, no. For a time I wondered about you. I worried, just a little . . .'

'No need,' she said. 'We were lucky that night to be so high up the mountain.'

'Ah,' he said. 'That night. A magic night.'

'A magic place,' she said. 'This place, I mean.'

'How did you know it was magic?'

'MacGregor told me. As a scientist I didn't believe him.'

'But now?'

'Oh yes, Graham. Yes, I believe him now.'

She moved in closer, raising her face.

So he kissed her.

So she raised her whole body towards him.

Below in the corrie the 12-pointer roared again.

'Do you know what MacGregor told me, Janet?' he asked, kissing her neck.

She moaned so that he knew she was too far gone to reply.

'He said that if you could only make love to the girl of your choice up here on the Tine when the Master stag was roaring down below, she would be true to you all your life.'

Janet moaned again and said thickly: 'Very unscientific, darling, but I don't feel very scientific. The zip's at the side,' she added.

For some minutes the 12-pointer belled though neither of them heard his roars. Later, when they both looked down from the Tine, Hulke had removed his shattered body from the corrie.

'At last we are alone,' Graham said.

'A magic place,' Janet said dreamily. 'Perhaps we ought to make doubly sure the magic works.'

They did so and when they looked down from the Tine the next time, a Royal Navy helicopter was setting down just behind the NERTS cottages.

'There they go,' Janet said. 'Sir Irwin and his bowler-hatted commandos.'

'At last, we are really alone,' Graham said again.

Janet kissed him but said firmly, 'Darling Graham. I am not a hind and you are not a stag.'

'Darling Janet. That's the most marvellous thing of all. How awful if we were condemned to a rutting season like the rest of them.'

Within an hour of the RAF landing them at Northolt, Sir Irwin and Raymond Braithwaite had made their report to the Prime Minister at No. 10. Only Sniffy Snettisham was absent. He had been hospitalised in a maximum security ward the moment the party had reached the mainland.

Almost as soon as Sir Irwin and Braithwaite had left, an urgent signal arrived from the Admiralty. Its contents had so shaken the Prime Minister that he had called an immediate Cabinet meeting.

The Prime Minister read the Navy's signal out slowly.

'Russian trawler *Kara* slipped through in a fog. Interception impossible. *Kara* put Dr Mathews ashore in a rubber dinghy in the Orkneys. A Coastguard found him wandering along the beach. Preliminary medical examination suggests that the Russians injected him with Pentathol to make him talk.'

The Prime Minister broke the long silence that followed.

'We have to consider the implications of what has taken

place on Horn. At its simplest, or again at its most complicated, we seem to have invented a method of channelling and concentrating the entire reproductive drive of the human race. It would appear that, through accidental exposure to radiation of a rare and hitherto unknown type, we have induced a disparate selection of human beings to conduct their reproductive functions within a strictly limited period, or, as Sir Irwin would call it, a rutting season. The point is: how do we view this development?'

'As a definite breakthrough, Prime Minister,' the Minister for Energy was eyes-ashine with innovative zeal. 'We have opened up new horizons for the human race.'

The Minister for Scottish Affairs said, 'You may want to go around butting everyone for one month of the year, but what the hell do you propose doing for the other eleven months?'

'Ah,' Illingworth was at his most earnest. 'That's the whole point. Just consider the amount of creative energy that the men of the country squander, day in and day out, in petty sexual jealousy and worrying about their virility. Try to recall on your own account, Prime Minister, what it was like when you were a young man.'

'I didn't go round butting people.'

'Speaking for myself,' Illingworth said, 'and I flatter myself that I wasn't entirely unattractive to the fair sex, I recall that I did put in a great deal of time on what was then often called courting. Moreover, I worried out of all proportion when my ventures came to nothing.'

'Pity he doesn't do so now,' muttered the Home Secretary.

'How much better it might have been, had I been able to concentrate all that worry, all that endeavour into one short period of the year. Who knows, I might have reached the top of my modest calling even earlier than I have actually done. What my Ministry now seems to have achieved is to make such a concentration of energy possible on a national scale.'

'What your Ministry has actually done, Ted,' said the Prime Minister, 'is to let a bloody great concentration of energy leak where nobody particularly wants it or needs it.'

The Home Secretary felt it was time he had his dig at the ever-unpopular Ted. 'Are you suggesting that the red-blooded young men of this country might welcome a whiff of your magic gas in order to deprive themselves of their favourite participant sport for all but thirty days of the year?'

'Think of the compensations, the advantage of being able to concentrate on their careers. The beneficial effect on national out-put.'

'Think of the chaos,' said the Home Secretary. 'Just imagine rutting stockbrokers charging each other, brief-case to briefcase, on Weybridge Station. All those voices breaking first downwards and then upwards. Everyone's skull itching.' The Home Secretary judged that the best way to shut Illingworth up was to play him for comedy. 'Neck and shoulder muscles swelling so that everybody suddenly splits the seams of their suits and shirts. I suppose there might be a good line for the rag trade in flogging rutting gear. "Get one two sizes larger for October." That kind of thing.'

The Minister for Scottish Affairs did not view universal rutting as a laughing matter. 'What you seem to be suggesting is dosing the whole nation with this poison you have inadvertently let loose on part of my homeland. If such a notion is even stirring in your cranium, all I can say is that if you didn't exist, George Orwell would have had to invent you.'

Illingworth filled his pipe. 'Oh come on. We're a long way from anything of the sort and, anyhow, there'd have to be a referendum first.'

'Thanks,' said the Prime Minister with heavy sarcasm. 'I'm glad you thought of that. Meantime perhaps we should consider how to deal with what is, mercifully, so far only a local problem.'

'Before we do so . . .' Audrey Margetson began.

The Prime Minister saw with alarm that she intended to make a speech.

'Before we do so, may I draw attention to the fact that the Minister for Energy totally, and I'm afraid, typically, ignored the advantages of a controlled mating season for women. Women have always been shackled to the needs of men.'

The Prime Minister rolled his eyes ceiling-wards. Audrey Margetson prattled on. 'What a vista would open up ahead of women, free of the needs to compete with other women for men's attentions. Doesn't Sir Irwin's report stress that very point, namely that, once the rut is over, all the females are likely to live in perfect harmony with each other? What might such united woman-power do!'

'Aye what?' said the Scotsman. 'It hardly bears contemplating.'

'Think of what women might accomplish during those sex-free eleven months of the year.'

'For nine of them, I should think they'd all be calving . . . I mean having babies.'

'There *is* such a thing as the pill.'

'If they remembered to take it. I imagine you could get out of the habit in eleven long, loveless months.'

The Prime Minister felt it was time to bring the meeting to order.

'Let us now consider what use the Russians can be expected to make of any information they may have extracted from Dr Mathews under drugs.'

'What,' asked the Home Secretary, 'are the Russians supposed to get out of the information, even if they can deduce enough to copy Ted Illingworth's blinding and unfortunate fluke and make some of this rutting gas of their own? Release it over NATO HQ, or even Peking, and then when all the four-star generals and high-up Chinks are butting the living daylights out of each other, launch a few hundred armoured divisions?'

Ted Illingworth came back fast.

'I'll tell you what they might do with it. Just exactly what I have been talking about. Use the stuff to increase production not only of war materials but consumer goods. *They'd* have no second thoughts about streamlining *their* work force, about getting all their sex over in one month so that they could turn out more tractors and sputniks in the other eleven.'

'I like it. I like it.' The Home Secretary was still busy putting the Minister for Energy down. 'Just imagine if it caught on here. It'd be a bit like Wakes Week. Fords, Dagenham, and British Leyland everywhere would have to close down for the rutting month . . . If they weren't on strike already, that is. Maybe we could persuade the TUC to hold all its strikes in October or whatever month we chose for our sexual jamboree.'

The Prime Minister winced. He didn't like jokes of any sort about strikes. It was time for a firm hand.

'Let us take it that whatever the Russians may have learned, we can do nothing to stop them. The Island of Horn is, however, our very grave responsibility. We will therefore adopt the following measures.

'First, secrecy must be maintained. No one will leave the island. Only persons authorised by myself will visit it.

'Second, NERTS, together with the Ministry of Health, will set up a small but efficient scientific study unit to monitor the, as it were, close season.

'Third, the Army's Tracking Unit will remain stood down.

'Fourth, every effort will be made to find an antidote to bring these unfortunate people back to normal.

'I want your respective recommendations on my desk within twenty-four hours. Sir Irwin Broadchalke and Dr Braithwaite are to be consulted in all your discussions. And Ted . . .'

'Yes, Prime Minister.'

'Is that Dundoom security chap . . . what's his name? . . .'

'Gilbey?'

'Yes, Gilbey. Is he still under observation?'

'Not only under observation but under lock and key.'

'Keep him that way. And Dr Mathews, too. Use them as guinea-pigs. But find the antidote.'

The Close Season

Graham knocked on Janet's door. She sat up sleepily in bed, naked as the moment at which he had left her in the early hours of the morning. She held out her arms lovingly.

'Graham, darling. How lovely. You don't usually . . .' Then as if suddenly remembering her nakedness she drew the covers up over her breasts. They made him think of Ben Dhui, in fact two Ben Dhuis. The gesture was more provocative than the breasts themselves which was saying a good deal. Not for the first time in the five days and nights that had passed since the magic surrender on the Tine, did Graham reflect on the wonderously uninhibited way this girl had given herself to him. The ice flower had taken a long time to melt but now that spring was at last here the unfolding and blooming was miraculous both to behold and experience. He felt himself to be wandering amidst a vast carpet of flowers.

Graham forced himself to resist the invitation to join her. Out of a strange sense of propriety, perhaps because they were, after all, still members of a NERTS scientific mission paid for, trusted and housed by NERTS, he always returned to his own bed in the next-door cottage two hours before dawn. He wondered, in fact they both wondered, how long such abstemiousness could last.

Who was to know or care? Hulke was up at the tracking base, a shattered man, totally exhausted by his excesses, collar bone broken and body severely bruised as a result of his encounter with the stag. Dr Whymper had him in her care. As for Fergus Roxborough, he had moved in with MacGregor, though neither appeared to seek the other's company. Dr Roxborough, too, was thoroughly debilitated. He barely acknowledged Graham or Janet apart from remarking that he had important work to do. Flora Flodden had asked to be taken on as part-time cook with the Army. It seemed she couldn't bear to be away from her female companions.

So Graham could quite easily have immediately hopped back into bed with Janet that morning, without anyone being the wiser, except that he had news to discuss with her in the form of a radio message just delivered from Captain Pomona's orderly room.

'It's marked "Highly Confidential" and it's from Sir Irwin. It says that you and I have been appointed to conduct a special study of post-rutting-season behaviour. "Repeat special."'

'We'd be doing that anyway, Graham.'

'"Repeat Special" can only mean one thing. Our study is not so much of *Cervus elephas*, as of *Homo sapiens*.'

'I see. Well we might as well start here. I do believe you're a sneaky rutter, Graham.'

'I'm no sort of rutter at all, thank God. I'm a healthy, normal, happily hetero member of the human race. And so are you, my love.'

'Prove it.'

'The message ends by saying that Sir Irwin and ourselves are personally responsible to the Prime Minister.'

'Graham . . .' The bed covers had been lowered again.

'Can't I impress you with anything, Janet?'

'Yes, Graham.'

'Oh very well,' he said. 'Just this once then.'

Captain Pomona could not understand what had come over himself or his command in the two months since everyone had returned exhausted to base, except that he knew that, whatever it was, it affected them all equally and had to be accepted. He no longer worried that his unit was, so to speak, off the air. Everyone was so preoccupied with new and surprising pursuits. Myfanwy Preece had developed a sudden interest in early Welsh history. Cardiff University was supplying her with a degree course by correspondence. He no longer felt any amorous interest in her or she in him, or any other him in any other her and vice versa. This sexual truce was deeply peaceful and seemed entirely natural. It did not even occur to him, or to anyone else, that they were missing something.

For the rest, Butch Cassidy and Hideous 007 Bond were studying *cordon bleu* cookery – one of the reasons he had been happy to accept Flora Flodden's services as supernumerary assistant cook. Some of the Cassidy-Bond experiments were definitely not the stuff to give the troops.

Joanna Bromley was at last writing the definitive book on gannets.

He himself was working on some advanced electronics, experimenting with a visual tracking system involving lasers and holographs. CSM Markham was constructing, with the aid of a little-known book by Sir Ralph Payne-Galwey, a full-sized Roman *ballista* with the object of hurling rocks across the Race of Horn at defenceless Hummel. He had always wanted to be in the Artillery.

The girls, Scots and English alike, had set up some very promising handicraft activities including tapestry, pottery and tweed weaving. Mavis Prendergast was turning out to be a very fair water colourist. Cecilia Munt was well into a complete flora collection of Horn's vegetation. Dr Janet Morgan and MacCallister had been very helpful there. Those two spent a lot of time at the army base, just talking to people in the most interested fashion. They were both very welcome, of course, but Pomona wished they wouldn't go on in quite the way they did, holding hands and so on. What was all *that* about? *So* unnatural. And so unnecessary.

Jeannie McCall had decided to take a course in local politics. The Scottish Nationalists had been glad to oblige her with instruction by post. Corporal Gunnersbury, very sensibly, in view of his natural talents, was studying brewing and home wine-making.

In furthering all these new interests, Captain Pomona amazingly received full and prompt co-operation from the authorities. The *Haddie* no longer called. Instead a fast Royal Navy patrol boat put in once a fortnight carrying not only food and drink but packages of instructional handbooks and materials, including seasoned oak for the *ballista*. She bore away with her crates of empties and piles of completed exercises on subjects varying from the life and times of Offa and his dyke, to samples of heather wine.

This sexless, cultural idyll had not been without its rough spots. For a week or two male voices had been inclined to crack into a falsetto or even a piping treble, but this had gradually sorted itself out and things were vocally more or less back to normal now. What would ordinarily have been an extremely rough moment in Captain Pomona's life was about to occur at this very second. Regina Whymper knocked timidly on his door and was bidden to enter.

'Come in, Regina.'

The MO was smiling broadly. Captain Pomona no longer feared a smiling or for that matter scowling Whymper.

'I've just been holding my weekly medical parade for the girls.'

'Well done.'

'They're pregnant.'

'What, all of them?'

'Every last one.'

'Most satisfactory.'

'And, Bertram.'

'Yes.' He was already re-engrossed in a laser circuit.

'Can't you guess?'

'You are, too.'

'Aren't you pleased?'

'Excellent,' he said. 'One hundred per cent breeding success. When do you all drop your calves, I mean give birth?'

'July. It's going to be a busy month.'

'Certainly is,' said Pomona without looking up.

One day, just before Christmas, Janet and Graham returned, depressed, from a routine visit to the Army. It looked as though Christmas was going to be a pretty dull affair at the Tracking Unit. The girls were planning to spend it together, without men.

'Exactly like a herd of pregnant hinds,' Janet had observed.

The men were obviously going to get solitarily drunk in

the NCO's mess. 'A stag party to the life,' Graham said.

Janet spoke little on the chilly walk back. But her silence was not entirely due to the Army's unseasonal Christmas prospects.

The air was frosty in more ways than one.

'What's wrong, darling?'

'Oh nothing.'

'Yes it is.'

'What did I say wrong?'

'You didn't *say* anything.'

'Oh.'

'No.'

'Then what did I do?'

'If you don't know, I can't tell you.'

They turned in at the cottage gate.

'Janet, you're picking a quarrel with me.'

'Well, you deserve it.'

'Oh do I, by God? How feminine, how typically feminine. You won't even say what upset you.'

'I saw you making sheep's eyes at Myfanwy Preece.'

'Oh don't be so bloody unscientific. You know she's incapable of feeling anything like that.'

'Yes, but you're not.'

'I never heard anything so ridiculous.'

Janet ran into their bedroom and slammed the door. Some time later, he heard her sobbing.

Graham waited a minute or two and then entered softly. Janet was lying red-eyed, staring at the ceiling.

'Oh, Jan,' he said. 'Oh, Jan. You couldn't really believe anything so crazy. You know it's you I love and always will.'

He picked her up in his arms and started kissing her moist eyelids. So they made love and afterwards she said to him: 'Oh, Graham, isn't it terrible for them all, the way they are up there. They don't know any more what a joy it is to quarrel and then make it up. I do love you so.'

The New Year came and so did Sir Irwin Broadchalke and Raymond Braithwaite. They spent two days at NERTS cottages which meant that Janet and Graham had hurriedly to move back to separate rooms. This did not, however, deceive Raymond Braithwaite who raised one of his charmer's eyebrows and remarked: 'I see everything's nice and normal, darlings. *Aren't* you lucky?'

Sir Irwin brought top secret news with him. The nuclear physicists at Dundoom had isolated the precise form of radiation that had caused the trouble. Moreover they appeared to think they could recreate it at will.

'What's the point of that?' Graham asked. 'Are they aiming to develop it as a secret weapon, or something?'

'Hardly that, MacCallister. But Raymond here seems to think that moderate exposure to same could reverse the hormonal imbalance.'

'You mean give 'em a second whiff and they'll all be okay again?'

'I didn't go as far as that, but some preliminary work is being done on Gilbey, the night watchman, who copped a packet at Dundoom.'

'And what about poor old Jerry Mathews?'

'When he's fully recovered psychologically from his experiences, Raymond may also try some controlled radiation treatment on him.'

'Good God. You mean you're treating Jerry like a laboratory rat.'

'Something has to be done for all these poor people,' Sir Irwin said. 'Seeing Captain Pomona today so morose and isolated like a hungry stag in winter quite upset me. And all those pregnant women!'

'Are you proposing to abort them all, Raymond?'

'On the contrary, Graham. They seem highly contented with their lot.'

'Let me see,' said Irwin, 'July's the month, isn't it? We'll have to get some extra accommodation built before then, a sort of crêche, no doubt. First time it's ever happened in the British Army, I dare say.'

When the patrol boat called to take Sir Irwin and Raymond Braithwaite off next day, the doctor said: 'All right, dears, you can rearrange the bedroom furniture again now.'

*

Raymond Braithwaite faced the Prime Minister across a glass of sherry.

'You really believe it will work?'

'Prime Minister. Let me just say that the first tests on Gilbey appear very promising. He's responding well to small doses of modified radiation. Dundoom have now been able to supply us with as much as we need of the source material.'

'What sort of response are you getting?'

'He became far less aggressive after the first dose. By the third exposure he was seen to be reading *Penthouse* and *Playboy* which have been left casually in his ward as a sort of blue litmus paper.'

'That *is* impressive. So what are you suggesting?'

'Long before October, I hope we'll be able to forecast whether a second dose for Horn will do the trick.'

'For the whole damn island?'

'That is the line we're working on at the moment.'

In early June Captain Pomona received a signal from the MOD telling him that the next visit by the patrol boat would bring a special prefabricated nursery building which his men would be required to erect.

Captain Pomona sent for CSM Markham and broke the news.

'It's going to break into our more important activities, sir.' The CSM sounded sulky but then he often did these days. His *ballista* was giving trouble. At the first attempt to bombard Hummel it had misfired, hurling a rock backwards over the cookhouse, greatly upsetting Butch Cassidy's *rum baba*.

'Can't help that, CSM. None of us wants to be interrupted in our work, but this comes direct from the MOD.'

'Can't the women do it themselves? After all, it's for their own good.'

'Sorry, CSM. They're in no condition.'

'I can see that, sir. Very noticeable. But the men won't like it, sir.'

'Then they'll have to do the other thing.'

'Very good, sir.'

The men most certainly did not like it. When the new building arrived, each section proved to be diabolically heavy.

'What's the bloody thing lined with?' Lance Corporal Mason complained. He was still having trouble with his damaged elbow. 'Lead?'

'Are you sure this lead foil of yours will keep it out?' the Prime Minister demanded. 'Those innocent unborn babes have got to be protected somehow. I don't want to be told in a year or so's time that you've created a group of infantile rutters. Just imagine a gang of toddlers all charging each other with high chairs.'

'I have it on the highest scientific authority, Prime Minister,' said Ted Illingworth, 'that they will be entirely protected in the new crêche building if, and when, we decide to give Horn a second treatment.'

'I'd like to shift them to the mainland. But I suppose we can't take them away from their mothers. They need special attention.'

'Those innocent unborn babes will need special attention and I'm going to see that they get it, Prime Minister.'

'Quite right, Audrey! What do you propose to do about it?'

'I intend to make a personal visit to Horn.'

'Excellent notion,' said the Prime Minister, who was appalled at the very idea. 'I'll arrange naval transport for you. I'd like your recommendations about posting experienced nursing staff to look after the babies while their mothers are . . . er . . . on duty. Especially during early October.'

'The Minister for Health's going to visit us,' announced Graham. 'I hear she's a bit of a man-eater.'

'Just keep your thieving eyes off her, then, Graham.'

'Jealous, Janet darling?'

'Thank your lucky stars I can produce a touch of the green-eyed monster. For some people, jealousy's an unheard of luxury. Or have you forgotten? Wonder what she wants.'

'Audrey Margetson? Apart from being a sex maniac I hear she's a raving feminist. Probably wants to see how women can do without men.'

'Horrible thought, darling Graham.'

'Horrible, Janet darling.'

Audrey Margetson was deeply impressed with everything she saw on Horn, especially the singlemindedness of the men in their chosen activities and the solidarity and fellow feeling that pervaded among the now all too pregnant women. She interviewed Regina Whymper, more spectacular than ever in her eighth month.

'You're going to need some medical assistance very soon, Doctor.'

'I'm sure we can manage very well, Minister. I *have* delivered babies before, you know.'

'Including your own?'

'Nature all around us manages very well. We could well learn from the deer for instance.'

'Quite, Dr Whymper. Nevertheless, the Army will be sending you an experienced midwife.'

'She'll have to be pretty good at her job. There could be a dozen or more babies all arriving at once.'

'Quite. That's why we sent you the crêche. The midwife will look after the babies at night. That's what the little room at the end of the new hut is for. After all, the mothers are still in the Army. We can't allow babies in the barrack room.'

The Minister approved of Graham, too.

'What a nice young man,' she said to Janet. 'You two, I believe, are quite, well, quite untouched.'

'Yes, thank heavens, Mrs Margetson.'

'Oh do call me Audrey.'

'Very well, Audrey.'

'I'd be interested in your opinion as a scientist, Janet. Don't you agree there could be great advantages to condensing all human sexual activity into one short period?'

'Can't think of one, Audrey.'
'As a woman, then?'
'I can't imagine anything worse.'

After the chopper had taken the Minister back to the mainland, Janet and Graham walked hand in hand along the cliffs. Graham lagged behind for a few minutes. When he caught Janet up he presented her with a large bunch of sea pinks.

'For you.'

'Oh, Graham, how old-fashioned and lovely. I wonder whether the Minister would approve. By the way, she had her eye on you.'

'Nonsense.'

'She did. A woman can tell. But then so have I. Come here.'

They lay down in a soft, heathery dell. A lark was singing somewhere high in the blue sky above.

'Sing your heart out, little man,' Graham said. 'Your spirit won't be blithe for very long.'

The midwife, a thirty-year-old member of the Middlesex Hospital's maternity department, arrived a week later. She had been carefully selected, screened and briefed by the Energy and Health Ministers in person. She had been placed under the Official Secrets Act and given sealed instructions only to be opened and acted upon on receipt of the code words 'Repeat Performance'. She had been told that the code words were not likely to be sent until late September or early October.

Until then her capable hands were more than full.

On July fifth, Mavis Prendergast gave birth, perhaps for sentimental reasons, in the equipment store. She was discovered an hour later rather like a cat who has her kittens in the airing cupboard, curled up in the blanket-lined parabolic aerial, scene of many a tender encounter with Lance Corporal Mason. The baby, a strapping boy, did not, however, resemble her lover of long-forgotten days. It, alas, reminded everyone of Hulke.

From then on, and mercifully fairly well spread over the

next ten days, Horn was bursting out all over. Butch Cassidy and 007 Bond dropped theirs out in the heather. Both daughters, the infants had more than a touch of CSM Markham about their beetling brows. Several of the Scots lassies paid tribute to MacGregor's success on the lekking ground. As Raymond Braithwaite, who had recently arrived as medical observer, had previously prophesied, the strength of the Clan MacGregor was about to be greatly increased on Horn.

Towards the end of the calving period, things hotted up considerably, so much so that Raymond Braithwaite, who hadn't dabbled in midwifery since his student days, found himself in it up to his elbows. The last batch of babies, unluckily for them, all bore the unmistakable mark of Hulke. This, in itself, was not surprising since the final phase of the rut was the period during which Hulke had achieved full dominance.

Throughout this litter of *accouchements* Dr Whymper remained a tower of strength delivering babies with the best of them until she finally succumbed herself, shedding her male calf with the ease of a red deer hind. Its wispy black hair suggested that Pomona had had a hand in the production though, allowing for his general lack of success during the rutting season, this was probably wishful thinking.

At the end of the day, or rather at the end of fourteen days, the score was, in the various estimations of Raymond Braithwaite, Janet and Graham:

Hulke: Eight to Ten.

MacGregor: Four.

Markham: Maximum Two.

Pomona: One, unconfirmed.

Roxborough & Mathews: Nil.

Mason & Gunnersbury did not run.

However, it was very hard to be certain.

Apart from the unhappy resemblance of the majority to Hulke, the babies were all perfectly normal.

The Prime Minister held regular fortnightly conferences on Situation Horn.

‘I have good news and I have bad news,’ the Minister for Energy began at the first August meeting.

‘First the bad news. The Prime Minister, is, of course, already privy to the facts. The rest of this meeting should know, however, that the Russians appear to have been carrying out some very unusual nuclear experiments. We can’t be sure but there is some indication that they are attempting to manufacture radioactive substances very similar to those that were responsible for the phenomena on Horn.’

‘I warned you,’ shrieked Audrey Margetson. ‘They won’t hesitate to rearrange the breeding habits of their entire population in order to become more efficient.’

‘Thank you, Audrey,’ said the Prime Minister icily. ‘Now may we have the good news?’

‘The good news is that treatment of both Gilbey, the night watchman, and Dr Mathews confirm that a second exposure to a slightly modified form of the radiation reverses the hormonal trend.’

‘You mean that they are returning to normal?’

‘Have practically returned, Prime Minister.’

‘So now we are in a position to give the whole island of Horn a second dose?’

‘Correct.’

The Prime Minister assumed his matters-of-national-gravity face.

‘This has to be my decision and my decision alone.’

Everyone felt glad about that. As for the Prime Minister he thought he knew how Harry Truman felt before he decided to drop the Bomb on Hiroshima.

‘Is Dundoom prepared to engineer a deliberate leak of this stuff on the chosen night?’

‘Quite ready, Prime Minister.’

‘Well let’s hope it works.’ The Prime Minister couldn’t resist a dig. ‘They’re good enough at accidental leaks.’

‘The rut should start by October first,’ Sir Irwin Broadchalke put in hastily. ‘That applies to Horn’s red deer and in this case, if all runs true to form, to the human rutters also. So Dundoom better be standing by from September twenty-fifth onwards.’

'We'll be ready,' said Ted Illingworth with his justly feared air of confidence.

The Prime Minister turned to the Air Ministry Met. man. 'We'll need one hundred per cent accurate weather forecasts, particularly about wind strength and direction.'

'From late September until mid-October the prevailing south-east wind on that coast is remarkably constant.'

'So choice of night depends on getting ideal weather conditions during the period in question?'

'Correct, Prime Minister.'

'And Captain Pomona understands his orders?'

The Brigadier said: 'Yes, he'll be told to take all personnel on a night exercise on the chosen date.'

'Good,' said the Prime Minister, 'it's very important that all the affected people are outdoors so that we achieve maximum exposure. By the way, what kind of a night exercise? I understand they're all engaged on basket-making and that sort of thing.'

'Pomona can be told that his people are to help NERTS on a lowground deer count,' Sir Irwin suggested.

'First class,' said the Prime Minister

Audrey Margetson asked petulantly: 'Why does it all have to take place at night?'

'Because,' said the Prime Minister equally petulantly, 'I feel far better if this kind of dirty work does take place at night.'

And that settled it.

In early September, Sir Irwin and Raymond Braithwaite paid a final visit to Horn.

Braithwaite inspected the crêche and, finding no horns or slotted feet on the babies, pronounced himself satisfied. Sir Irwin briefed Captain Pomona on the importance of all his troops plus civilian supernumeraries – Hulke and Roxborough and MacGregor had now moved in with the army – being out on the hill to assist in a deer count on receiving orders from the MOD. Pomona was almost enthusiastic. Sir Irwin wondered if, perhaps, this was because the rutting juices were beginning to stir in him.

Finally Sir Irwin talked to Janet and Graham.

‘I think you ought to leave.’

‘We’ll be okay. We were before.’

‘Where?’

‘This time we’ll both be out of harm’s way in the cup on top of the Tine.’

‘Can Janet get there?’

‘She’s been there already.’

‘Zero hour will be midnight. Take care, then.’

‘We will. We’re too happy as we are.’

‘Yes,’ said Sir Irwin in a rare moment of sentimentality. ‘I believe you are.’

It was once again the night of the full moon. The message ‘Repeat Performance’ had come through at 1800 hrs.

Captain Pomona sent for CSM Markham.

‘That night exercise I told you about. It’s tonight. I want everyone out on the low ground, counting deer, by 2000 hours. They’re not to return until 0230. Apparently it’s very important.’

The CSM saluted more smartly than he’d done for some time. He seemed quite keen to be out there with the stags again. Everyone had already heard the first roarings.

‘And CSM.’

‘Sir.’

‘The nursing sister. She’s the only one to stay behind. To look after the babies. She’s got some sealed orders. She’s to open them now.’

At 2000 hrs, just as the Army contingent was setting out, Graham kissed Janet and said: ‘This is it. Let’s go. It’ll take us two hours to make the climb.’

The sky was clear and the moonlight so bright the heather seemed again to be touched with frost. A steady breeze was scudding a solitary cloud along towards the north-west. They climbed in silence. When they reached the rock wall at the base of the Tine they heard a big stag roaring.

‘The twelve-pointer,’ Graham said.

She took his hand. He could feel the excitement in her finger tips.

Ten minutes later, they were through the drain hole at

the top of the Tine and had wriggled into the cup. The time was 2150 hrs.

'In ten minutes,' he said, 'Dundoom will make its release.'

Far away he could pick out the two red snake's eyes that were the warning lights on top of Dundoom's chimneys.

Somewhere, down below them in the moonlit heather, Captain Pomona and his troops kept their watch for the deer which, unknown to themselves, they still resembled.

In their lead-lined hut the innocent man-calves of Horn slumbered safely.

Far, far away to the East, Russian nuclear scientists were, perhaps near to success. Who could tell?

'A magic night,' said Graham. 'Just like the full moon of the rut a year ago.'

'Except that I wasn't here.'

'You are now.'

Below them the master stag roared again.

'You know what they say about hearing that stag. The magic works for life.'

'Make doubly sure, then, Graham.'

So he did.

Seventy-five miles away at Dundoom, a tiny puff of smoke appeared above each of the red snake's eyes and was snatched away on the strong wind towards the north-west.

In No. 10 the Prime Minister looked at his watch. Ten p.m. The moment of truth.

He didn't often talk to himself, largely because in his line of work there was always someone to talk at. But now he said out loud: 'I hope to God the wind doesn't change.'

He muttered a brief, silent prayer, not so much for the Island of Horn, but for the rest of sleeping Britain.

Then, to the surprise of the duty policeman, he went outside, stood in the middle of Downing Street, wet his finger and held it up to the wind.

Sometimes, he felt, the whole business of Government was just like that.

OFFICE LIFE

BY KEITH WATERHOUSE,
bestselling author of BILLY LIAR

OFFICE BUREAUCRACY LAID BARE!

From the ranks of the nation's clerks, Clement Gryce has surfaced from redundancy to join the working force at British Albion. The Stationery Supplies department on the seventh floor is Gryce's new billet and his colleagues – particularly the lovely Miss Divorce – seem just the ticket. Duties are light, not to say minimal.

Even so, there's something strange about British Albion. What does the company actually do? Why don't the telephones ever ring? Why does Lucas of Personnel make mysterious enquiries about Gryce's political beliefs? And why are two entire floors devoted to issuing luncheon vouchers for the staff canteen? The suspense is too much for Gryce, he decides the matter needs investigation and sets forth on a voyage of discovery all his own . . .

Anyone who has ever worked in the world of 'top-copy-and-two-carbons' will recognize the lunacies of office bureaucracy laid bare in this brilliantly savage lampoon.

And don't miss Keith Waterhouse's hilarious novel
JUBB
also available in Sphere Books

GENERAL FICTION 0 7221 0522 3 £1.25